MY SAFARI
A SON'S REVENGE

JAMES KNIGHT

© 2022 James Knight

All rights reserved. This book or any portion thereof may not be reproduced or used in any manner whatsoever without the express written permission of the publisher except for the use of brief quotations in a book review.

Print ISBN: 978-1-66785-736-7
eBook ISBN: 978-1-66785-737-4

1.

MY SAFARI BEGAN THE day my mother died.

She died of a broken heart.

She was a remarkable woman, a world traveler who never ventured far from the small Virginia island where she was born. She was a traveler of the heart and the mind and the spirit, and in her kind and patient way she took me places found only in the imagination.

I was born, Jackson Andrew Quill, in Broadwater, a small village on Hog Island off the coast of Virginia. It was a Tuesday, a day known all over the world as Black Tuesday, October 29, 1929, the day the stock market crashed. The Great Depression crippled a lot of businesses, including my father's oyster business in Hog Island Bay. But my mother, the eternal optimist, thought when things got worse, they had to get better. Her entire life was based on wishful thinking. It would be the death of her.

In August 1933, a hurricane with winds over a hundred miles an hour slammed into Hog Island with such force it demolished houses, boats, ripped out trees, even washed away shorelines. It destroyed a post office, general store, a school, a church, all supported by 250 people and a thriving oyster trade with fleets of boats and shucking houses. To the hardworking men and women of Broadwater, Hog Island was heaven on earth. But that day ended their way of life. And it wrecked my father's pride and joy, the Molly Jean, his faithful oyster buy-boat, our livelihood. After that, he was never the same.

As usual, my mother believed it to be an omen of better days to come. Her optimism controlled her logic. My father saw things differently. Wishful thinking was not enough to improve matters. That took action, not belief.

When the storm passed, my mother and father, drenched and exhausted, saved as much of their belongings from our shattered home as they could. We boarded one of the ferries carrying survivors to Willis Wharf, eleven miles across Hog Island Bay. My parents moved into a small clapboard house on the mainland, hoping to return to Broadwater and salvage what was left of our home. Some twenty-five structures were still intact enough to load onto barges to be shipped across the bay. Our house was not one of them. It had too much damage. They left it to rot with the rest of the abandoned houses. Ten years after the big hurricane, most of those who lived on Hog Island had moved to the mainland. The ocean claimed the land, and the graveyards gave up its dead to the sea.

Life in Willis Wharf proved difficult for my family, especially for my father. He had been an oyster man long before I was born. It took him years of working as a crew member on skipjacks to save enough money to get his own buy-boat. It was a beauty. Fifty feet long, painted white with a blue stripe running the length of the waterline. He named it the Molly Jean after my mother. In its heyday, it had a crew of three men gathering oyster hauls from skipjacks and delivering the daily harvest to wholesalers at Willis Wharf. He was really proud of that boat. When the great storm of 1933 sunk the Molly Jean, he turned bitter, cursing nature for the hand it had dealt him. There's still a plank from the boat somewhere around the house with the name Molly Jean on it.

Once my parents settled at Willis Wharf, the only work my father could find was as a shucker with Ballard Brothers Fish and Oyster Company. He worked for wages barely enough to support us. It was dirty, grueling work slicing the muscle from oyster shells with sharp knives that could cut a shucker's finger off. He'd come home smelling of sea grime, his hands black with dirt from hundreds of shells.

He suffered the shucking job for three years. Mother said he couldn't take it anymore. It wasn't because the job was hard and didn't pay much. Being around the oyster business was a daily reminder of the life he had lost as the owner of his own oyster boat. A life that was gone forever. The only job he could find was working at the Virginia zoo. He told my mother shoveling elephant shit was a promotion from shucking oysters.

I loved his job at the zoo. When I was old enough, he took me for a visit. The first animal he introduced me to was the biggest in the zoo. I must have been about six years old when I met my first elephant. Dad took me into the enclosure where they kept it. Her name was Betty and when we entered the pen she turned and started walking directly toward me. I remember screaming and jumping into my father's arms. He laughed when I buried my face in his chest, crying in fear. I remember feeling something tickling my neck. Dad turned me around just as this big gray trunk was inches from my nose. "This is Betty," he said. Betty let out a low rumble, her trunk searching me for something. "She wants a treat." Dad set me down and told me not to move. He didn't have to worry about that. I was petrified.

I stood stiff as a board until he found a bucket of apples and handed me one. "Go ahead," he said, "she loves apples." I reached out to give it to her, but my hand was shaking so hard I dropped it. Betty picked it up and pushed it toward me. "She wants you to give it to her." When I offered it to her, she let out a sound like a trumpet, curling her trunk over her head before taking it from me as gently as if she were taking a baby bird. "Okay," Dad said, "I'll be right back. Give her all she wants." He left me alone with a giant that could have crushed me flat with one foot. But Betty sat, waiting for more apples. She took about a dozen before letting out a long huff of wind that almost blew the baseball cap off my head. When my father returned, Betty was on her side. She was asleep. I sat staring at her. It was the beginning of a long friendship between me and this gentle soul.

I spent a lot of time at the zoo. Mr. Nagata, the director, taught me about the animals. He'd been to Africa several times to get animals for the zoo. He was an experienced zoologist. Been on several safaris. As a kid who had never been out of Virginia, I knew nothing about safaris. Mr. Nagata explained it meant to go on a journey. Tourists in Africa got in land cruisers which were trucks and drove around viewing wild animals. Some were hunters who hired guides to help them find and kill lions and elephants and bring them home as trophies. He said these people would skin the animals, have them stuffed, then hang them on their walls. He was against that. He said the killing of animals for sport was a sin against nature.

When he wasn't working at the zoo, Dad spent a lot of time with me. He helped me with my homework, played catch with me on the weekends, never missed any of my baseball games. And the books. Like my mom, he and I read a lot of adventure stories together, especially about Africa.

I became so interested in Africa I told my father I wanted to go there one day like the famous adventurer, Henry Stanley. It was my dad who bought me the book *How I Found Livingstone* by Henry Morton Stanley. It's a great story about how Mr. Stanley found Doctor Livingstone in a small remote village in Africa. I was at the age when boys longed for adventure. I spent an entire summer reading the Stanley book, underlining passages, discussing it with my father.. I would go on and on at the dinner table about Stanley and Livingstone until I was told to stop. So, I pestered my father to read to me at bedtime about their exploits.

Dad and I planned expeditions together. I got a notebook and made endless lists about the equipment I would take. I drew my own maps, tracing the path Stanley took on his journey over the savannas and through the jungles. But of all their exploits, it was the meeting between Mr. Stanley and Doctor Livingstone that captivated my imagination.

After years Stanley spent searching for Livingstone, enduring disease, floods, droughts, starvation, even considering suicide, he finally faced the man he'd risked his life to find, Doctor David Livingston. It was this famous true story about how a religious man, Doctor Livingston, went to Africa and when he didn't come home, everyone thought he might be dead. That's when this reporter, Henry Stanley, went looking for him. And when he found him, the words he spoke became a part of African history. I recited the words a hundred times that Stanley said to Doctor Livingston when he found him in a small African village in Tanganyika called Ujiji. The reports of that famous greeting spread around the world in 1871, exciting decades of other kids like me who dreamed of adventure. That simple greeting, "Doctor Livingstone, I presume," held all the mysteries of Africa for me.

The phrase became a thing between me and Dad. I even had my parents buy me a safari outfit, pith helmet and all so I could act out the meeting between Stanley and Livingstone in front of my bedroom mirror. I remember times when my father and I would read the story together. We'd lower our voices, and with our attempt at British accents, repeat, "Doctor Livingstone, I presume?" We got a big kick out of that. It's the fondest memory I have with my dad.

I haunted the library, looking for more books about the dark continent. I was eight years old when I discovered Osa Johnson's book, *I Married Adventure*. It was about this woman who married an adventurer, Martin Johnson, and how they explored Africa on safaris. They shot a lot of motion pictures. I saw them in newsreels when I went to the movies. I read a bunch of other books about Africa, too many to mention.

Those were the best years I had with my father, the years when he worked at the zoo. But his job there began to change him. He seemed to grow more and more restless. Became irritable, impatient. Stopped reading to me. He would be gone for days on end. We never knew where he went. Being a kid, I didn't know what was wrong with him. It turned out he couldn't accept being nothing more than an employee at a zoo. I overheard my mother telling her sister Edith that J.A. couldn't get over losing his big dream of becoming an oyster tycoon. I didn't know what a tycoon was. When I asked Mother about it, she said it meant he wanted to be a big shot in the oyster business. I didn't know what being a big shot meant. Then she explained to me my father's dreams were just too grand for him. I gave up trying to understand about tycoons and big shots and dreams that were too grand. You could fill a baseball stadium with things kids don't understand about grownups.

Then one day --- that day --- when my father came into my room early in the morning with his old army surplus backpack slung over his shoulder, I knew something was wrong. It was a workday, and he never came home in the middle of a workday. And he never wore his backpack to work. He leaned against the wall, stared at me with a funny look on his face. Came over and messed up my hair like adults do. Then he said, "Take care of your mother, buddy." Without another word, he walked out the door. I'll never forget the sound of the door closing. He might as well have slammed it in my face.

Later, I found Mom in the kitchen, crying. She was holding a note he'd written to her. The note was scribbled on a page from one of my blue-lined school notebooks. She wiped her nose on a tissue as she read it. It said, Dear Molly. Sorry I have to leave you. Off to find my fortune. Will be home soon with riches beyond imagination. Will keep in touch. J.A.

It would be almost eleven years before I saw him again.

2.

AFTER MY FATHER ABANDONED us, we soon ran out of money. My dad was our only means of support. To make ends meet, Mom had to borrow from her sister to pay the rent and buy food. That money didn't last long. So, mother took a job at the local post office sorting mail.

Not long after Dad took off, Mr. Nagata showed up at the house asking about him. He said when my father failed to come to work he worried something had happened to him. Mother made some lame excuse he had to go visit some relatives. When he kept questioning her, she finally broke down crying and ran out of the room. That's when I told Mr. Nagata my father didn't go to see any relatives. He was going on an adventure to find his fortune. I told him I didn't know when he was coming home. Mr. Nagata smiled and said I could come visit him at the zoo any time. And when I got a little older to come see him for a job.

After almost a year of being gone, it became obvious my father wasn't coming back. He wrote a lot of letters to us from places all over the world. He kept promising to send money, but none ever came. The letters my mother received were all about his so-called adventures. You'd think it would've made her angry that he left us destitute. But she seemed excited at the prospect he would find his fortune and come home with bags of gold and diamonds and piles of cash like he promised.

Often, my father would draw pictures in the margins of his letters, scribbled likenesses of the natives and artifacts in places he claimed to be exploring. He would include recipes for exotic foods from distant lands. When my mother could find the ingredients for these bizarre recipes, we would suffer bravely through meals unfit for civilized tastes.

Sometimes, in addition to letters, he would send packages containing such gruesome objects as a dried Piranha from the snake-infested waters of the Amazon, or the claws of a polar bear from the freezing wilderness of the North Pole. One time—and this was almost too much even for my mother's adventurous spirit—a shrunken head from the jungles of Ecuador.

She would often make remarks about how much she admired my father for his courage in following his dream. She once told me he was a great man, and someday historians would write about him like they wrote about all the great adventurers in history.

As time went on, I started worrying about her obsession that my father would someday come home with a fortune. We would sit out on our screened porch as she read his letters to me. She became so engrossed in my father's accounts of his worldly explorations she would faithfully read each page as if she had just received the first draft of a famous novel.

She became so caught up in the romance of my father's reported exploits she began to compare them to those of famous adventurers. She would retire to the screened porch on warm summer nights where she would sit in her rocking chair with me curled up on the floor beside her while she read from great books of legendary explorers. Together, we suffered the hardships of Crusoe in Daniel Defoe's *The Life and Adventures of Robinson Crusoe*, followed Jim Hawkins in his search for Captain Flint's buried treasure in Robert Louis Stevenson's *Treasure Island*, and Allan Quartermain's expedition through darkest Africa in pursuit of the legendary *King Solomon's Mines*.

It was all very exciting to her. But when my father wrote long flowery paragraphs about how much he missed my mother and me, that's when I resented him the most for abandoning us. What kind of father would leave his family destitute and then write home that he missed them? But she would just smile and say, "You remind me of him, Jack, and someday I hope you will grow up to be as brave a man as he is." No matter how much she tried to convince herself he still loved us and would come home someday, after he left, I had a bad feeling that he really didn't want to come back home. It was then I swore the day would come when I would find him and punish him for breaking my mother's heart.

3.

WHEN THE LETTERS FROM my father stopped coming, Mother worried something terrible had happened to him. The last one was from British East Africa, Kenya. His scrawled handwriting on stationery from a hotel called the Norfolk dated April 1, 1945. Mother answered with a long letter about how we missed him and how she needed him to come home. The letter was returned in a few weeks stamped "Addressee not at address."

Mother contacted the state department in Washington inquiring if they had heard of any foul play coming to an American in British East Africa. After many months, we received a letter from a Mr. Dankin, assistant to the under-secretary of state. He told us the British government reported that an investigation concerning a Mr. J.A. Quill had produced no information regarding a missing American in East Africa. My mother's fear turned to silent resignation. Although she continued to believe he was still alive and would someday return home, the constant worry about him took its toll. She stopped reading to me. She would sit alone on the porch, rocking her life away, clutching his faded letters, staring into an empty sky. The light in those sparkling eyes faded and the spirited voice I so depended on fell silent.

By my senior year in high school, my mother's health began to suffer. It became so serious she was forced to give up her job at the post office because of her fits of coughing and fainting. At one point, a coworker found her collapsed over a mail bin, unconscious and non-responsive. They rushed her to the hospital and diagnosed her condition as advanced emphysema.

Her doctor, Doctor Parks, ordered her to stay home for an extended period of bedrest. My Aunt Edith insisted on staying with my mother during the day. That meant I had to take a job to support us. So, I accepted Mr. Nagata's offer to work at the zoo.

It took me a good two hours to get to work from Willis Wharf to the mainland where the Virginia zoo was located. I would get up at 5 a.m., make breakfast for Mother, then head out for my ride on the Little Creek-Kiptopeke Beach Ferry across Chesapeake Bay to Virginia Beach.

Mr. Nagata gave me father's old job. After a year of feeding and taking care of the animals, they had gotten to know me pretty well. The zoo had three African lions, a male and two females. When I arrived at dawn every morning to feed them, the male lion would let out a roar of recognition. I don't know if it meant he liked me or he was just hungry. All the other animals took notice of my daily appearance. My feeding rounds meant lions roaring, zebra rushing to get their daily alfalfa, giraffe stretching necks over the fence for a mix of acacia leaves and carrots. And, of course, my longtime friend, Betty, the elephant.

Every morning when I appeared at her enclosure, she let out a brassy sound so loud it rattled her cage. I always made sure she had her fill of straw and vegetables, fruit, and a lot of water. And, of course, apples. I was the only one she let ride her. It drove the visiting kids wild to see me atop that magnificent creature.

When I got home at night, I would find Mother lying in her sickbed, staring at the ceiling. After Aunt Edith fed her and left to go home, I would read to her from the books of Edgar Rice Burroughs. Mother seemed to enjoy the exploits of *Tarzan of The Apes*. One time, when Tarzan was rescuing Jane, she said, "Someday my Tarzan will come swooping down from the trees to rescue me." As unlikely as that was, the thought seemed to give her a moment of hope.

By my 22nd birthday, Mother's health had gotten so bad Aunt Edith moved in with us to watch over her. The emphysema had taken a toll on my mother's ability to care for herself. She could no longer get out of bed without help. She had trouble feeding herself. Aunt Edith did her best to take care of her, but Mother's condition seemed to get worse each day.

Then came the day every son dreads. It was a Friday, and I had a busy day at the zoo, making sure the animals would have enough food for the weekend. It was dinnertime for the animals. When I approached the lion pen, Oscar, the big male, let out a roar that shook the ground.

"Easy boy," I told him. "I've got others to feed you know."

Oscar relaxed and sat on his haunches, staring up at me like a big kitten begging for food. As soon as I pitched a bucket of sirloin into the pen, the beast in him came alive. He pounced on the meat, growling viciously at the two females who timidly approached for their share. The bigger female, Missy, steered clear of Oscar. She came toward me.

"Don't worry, Missy. I haven't forgotten you."

I threw her a choice cut. She grabbed it and ran to a corner of the enclosure where the other female followed, fighting for her share of dinner.

"Morning, Jack."

Mr. Nagata always came to say hello during feeding time.

"Morning, sir."

I threw the rest of the meat into the cage. A violent scuffle exploded between Oscar and Missy for the last scrap of food. Missy took a powerful swipe at his head and connected. He backed away. I yelled at Oscar to leave her alone. He turned on me and growled.

"One of these days," Mr. Nagata said, "that guy will jump out of the pen and take your arm off."

"Nah. He loves me."

"You know, watching you with these animals reminds me of when your father worked here. They loved him too."

Mr. Nagata hadn't spoken my father's name since J.A. disappeared. Just the mention of his name made me angry.

"So, how's your mother?" he asked.

"Not good."

"Sorry to hear that."

We watched the lions for a moment.

"Any news from your father?"

Oscar ripped the last piece of meat to shreds.

"You mind if I take off early?"

"No, Jack. Just make sure everything's set for the weekend."

"All taken care of," I told him.

When I handed Mr. Nagata the empty bucket, Oscar let out another menacing growl. Mr. Nagata upended the bucket of the last scraps of meat and stared Oscar down.

"Don't start with me."

4.

I WAS BONE TIRED by the time I stepped off the ferry at the Kiptopeke pier. The sun was already at my back. I was anxious to get home before dark. The bus hadn't arrived, so I caught a ride with a man in a beat-up old truck. When we exchanged names, he said he knew my father. Said he had done business with him back in the day. He told me how he had been in the oyster business. He'd owned a skipjack before the '33 hurricane. Then he went on a rant about how the oyster business wasn't what it used to be what with the hurricane that ruined the oyster beds with too much freshwater runoff. By the time I got home, I'd heard enough about the history of oysters. I never really liked them.

When I saw two cars parked in front of the house, I knew something was wrong. One belonged to Aunt Edith. The other to Doctor Parks. He hadn't been to the house in a while.

Aunt Edith and the doctor were in my mother's bedroom. Aunt Edith had a chair pulled up to Mother's bedside. She was talking in whispers. The doctor sat on the other side of the bed. He was taking Mother's temperature. Aunt Edith jumped up when she saw me, her face streaked with tears.

"Jack. I'm glad you're home."

"What's going on?"

The room was darker than usual, smelling of medicine and sickness. When Mother saw me, she gave me a weak smile.

"My baby. Come here."

She reached out to me with arms so weak she could barely lift them. I sat beside her. She pulled me close. I asked her how she was feeling. I didn't know what else to say.

"I've been better."

Her arm shook as she tried to reach the nearby nightstand. She pointed.

"In the drawer. Hand me the letter," she said.

I gave her the letter. I'd seen it before. The same letter that had been in her nightstand for years. She took it in her hands, kissed it. Her eyes closed as if she was praying. When she spoke, her voice was strained, her words forced.

"It's from your father. Bless him. He's coming home soon, Jack."

She looked at me, her eyes full of tears.

"I was so afraid I would never see him again," she said. "But then the letter came, and I knew he was alive and well. Everything's going to be okay now."

I was about to tell her the letter was six years old, but Aunt Edith knew what I was thinking and shook her head.

"This is great, Mom," I said.

She coughed.

"Read it to me, son."

"Later, Mom. You need to rest now."

She tried to sit up.

"Take me out on the porch. Like we used to. We'll read it together."

I made her lie down. I stroked her hair, trying to calm her.

"Okay. I'll read it to you."

I glanced at Aunt Edith who stood in the corner, quietly sobbing.

I opened the worn envelope and took out the letter. As I read, Mother smiled, closed her eyes.

"Dearest Jack and Molly," I read. "I am writing about something that happened to me in the deepest and darkest part of Africa. I traveled to Tanganyika from Nairobi on safari to investigate a rumor about diamonds in a cave covering the ground like scattered rocks. We encountered a herd of buffalo on the salt flats south of the Mara River when out of the bush an angry rhino charged our party. My guide Makau turned in time to fire but his weapon jammed. Sadly, the rhino gored him to death. But I jumped free, falling down a hill into the river."

Mother's chest heaved. She coughed. A drop of blood dripped from her nose. The doctor pulled a handkerchief from his coat and wiped the blood away. I could tell she was in a lot of pain. She looked at me and nodded to continue.

"It was almost dark," I went on, trying to block out my mother's pain as I continued my father's unbelievable story. "I tried to swim. Heard the crocodiles coming for me. I had to make it to shore before I became their..."

Mother erupted in a violent fit of coughing so intense her chest shook in convulsions. She clutched her throat, gasping for air. The doctor took a syringe from his bag and gave her a shot. I jumped up, stood helplessly as she struggled to breathe.

The Doctor said, "I gave her a sedative. This will ease her pain."

It took a few minutes for the medication to take effect. I held her hands. They were cold. The doctor motioned me toward the door. Aunt Edith took my chair and started rubbing my mother's hands. I followed the doctor outside to the porch.

"Doc, how bad is she?"

"She's in the end-stage of emphysema."

"What does that mean?"

"Jack, she doesn't have long."

"But we can get her to a hospital. She'll be okay. Right?"

"It wouldn't help. Besides, she left instructions she wanted to be at home when she passed."

A stiff breeze blew in from the ocean strong enough to push the rocking chair back and forth. This was the chair where she would read to me so many nights about the exploits of the great adventurers. The same chair where she desperately read the letters from my father, hoping he would return someday. The creaking sound it made spooked me as if her soul had already left her body and was waiting there to read to me one last time.

The Doctor said, "Jack, is there any way to get in touch with your father?"

I could hear my mother's heavy breathing.

"What?"

"Can you get hold of your father?"

I shook my head. My mind focused on Mother and the possibility of losing her. The Doctor put a hand on my shoulder. Years of watching her suffer filled my thoughts.

I stared into darkness. "Is there anything you can do to save her?"

He shook his head.

We stood for a moment, locked in thought. There were no words of comfort that would soften the blow that my mother was dying. The Doctor shook my hand.

"I've got to be going, Jack. Your aunt has my phone number." He paused. "Just sit with your mother and make her comfortable."

He left. As he drove away, Aunt Edith joined me on the porch.

"She's asleep now," she said. She wiped away tears. "I'm glad you read her the letter. Those letters from your father gave her such hope through the years."

"Yeah," I said, fighting back anger. "Hope that eventually turned to hopelessness when she finally accepted that his letters were all lies."

"You knew they were lies?"

I laughed. "Of course. I knew long before she did. All those letters about headhunters in Ecuador, Amazonian lost tribes, expeditions to the North Pole. He'd drop names of famous adventurers he claimed to know. Hemingway, Heyerdahl, Sir Edmund Hillary." Aunt Edith and I exchanged knowing glances. "Aunt Edith, I'm not stupid."

"I know," she said. We were near enough to the ocean that we could hear the foghorns. "When did you find out?" she asked.

"I was about fourteen. We got a package one day from the Fiji Islands. I was lucky enough to open it before Mother got home. In it was a bula shirt. You know what bula means?"

She shook her head.

I told her, "I remember running to the library to look it up. It's how people in the Fiji Islands say hello. It's also a way they wish you happiness and good health." I saw the distant lights of a passing ship. "There was a letter in the package addressed to me. He told this story about how he took the shirt off a pirate who had attacked him on the high seas. According to him, he killed the pirate and jumped ship in time to avoid the other pirates killing him. He claimed he swam twenty miles to Fiji, barely avoiding being eaten by sharks. He said the bula shirt had given him good luck."

We watched the gray clouds hovering over the sea.

"But what made you think the story wasn't true?"

"I found a price tag on the shirt. Two dollars from a Fiji souvenir shop called Brown & Joske."

Aunt Edith buried her face in her hands. "Oh, God, Jack, I'm so sorry." She gave me a big hug. "And you never told your mother?"

"I didn't have the heart."

"Where's the shirt?"

"I threw it away."

A faint sound came from inside the house. A cough. Then gasping. A gurgling scream.

We hurried into the bedroom. My mother sat upright in bed, her body shaking violently, her eyes wide with fear. She tried to smile. She fell back. Her body contorted in pain, shaking uncontrollably. As quickly as it happened, it stopped. She wasn't breathing.

I frantically searched for medication, something to revive her. My Aunt got on the bed and put her mouth over Mother's mouth, trying to breathe air into her lungs. She did that until Mother's body went limp. Aunt Edith, breathless from her attempt to save her sister, finally gave up. We stared at my mother's lifeless body for a long time. Finally, my aunt looked at me, tears streaming down her face.

"She's gone, Jack."

In my mother's hand, the letter from my father, clutched tightly in a death grip.

5.

MY MOTHER'S LAST WILL and testament directed she was to be buried on Hog Island. But the island had been claimed by the sea and abandoned by the late 40s. We had no choice but to bury her in the Cape Charles cemetery about twenty miles southwest of Hog Island. We found a spot for her at the western end beneath a magnolia tree.

It was a brisk December day. The sun struggled with a few morning clouds but appeared in time for Mother's late afternoon funeral. Over 200 people gathered to see her off. All the former island residents that had moved to Willis Wharf from Hog Island after the '33 storm remembered the kind lady who handled their mail and whose husband had left her for parts unknown.

The Pastor from a local church conducted a brief service I didn't approve of. I resented any mention of my father.

"We are gathered here today," the Pastor began, "in remembrance of one Molly Quill who had a good life on the Barrier Islands where she was born. Through all her struggles, she was a good and kind person and a wonderful mother to her son, Jack. And to the end she kept a vigil for the love of her life, Jonathan Allen Quill, having faith her devoted husband who endured the hardships of his travels throughout the world would someday return to her with love and the riches she so deserved." I ignored the rest of his sermon, choosing to watch the clouds drift by. When I shifted uncomfortably, Aunt

Edith squeezed my arm as a reminder she also knew the heartache her sister had endured at the hands of my father.

The Pastor finished by acknowledging my mother's friends who attended the ceremony. "There's an old Irish saying that goes like this: May your home always be too small to hold all your friends. And counting the many friends of Molly Quill present here today, her home would be overflowing with those who loved her. Bless Molly Quill and may she rest in peace."

After the ceremony, Aunt Edith and I remained at the gravesite. The crowd had gone home, leaving us alone to pay our last respects to my mother. I stood with my arm around my aunt as a cold wind from the Atlantic scattered leaves over the modest stone marking my mother's grave.

The Pastor joined us. He expressed his condolences. Aunt Edith excused herself, reminding me of the reception to be held later at the house. The Pastor stood with me for a silent moment before speaking.

"Jack, although she attended my church from time to time, I didn't have the honor of knowing your mother very well. But friends of hers told me she was very proud of you. It's my understanding when she fell ill you took a job on the mainland to take care of her. Not many boys your age would assume such a responsibility."

I thanked him. He seemed pleased with himself. He should have stopped there.

"When was the last time you saw your father, Jack?"

I turned on him with such a vengeance, it startled him.

"Look, Pastor. Let's get something straight. My father's not a good man. He left me and my mother destitute. For years he wrote letters to her, lying about his adventures. Promising to come home someday with riches beyond imagination. He's never going to return. He never planned to return. It was all lies. I watched her struggle for years, wishing and hoping he would come home. When she finally realized he wasn't, it broke her. I will never forgive him for what he did to her. You know what she died from?"

The Pastor frowned. "I think it was emphysema."

"No, Pastor. She died from a broken heart."

That took a moment for him to process. I eased off.

"So, what do you plan to do with your life now?" he asked.

"I'm going to Africa."

"Africa? What's in Africa?"

"I think that's where my father is. I'm going there to find him."

I knelt, touched the stone above my mother's head. The inscription read: In loving memory of Molly Jean Quill. July 8, 1901–December 20, 1951. To know her was to love her.

6.

AFTER THE FUNERAL CEREMONY, I showed up for the reception to tell Aunt Edith what I planned to do. She understood, assured me she would take care of everything while I was gone, then slipped me a hundred dollars. I packed my gear and headed for the zoo.

It was after dark when I arrived. I'd never been to the zoo at night. It was spooky. The animals were mostly quiet except for the lions. As I passed their den, I felt I was being watched. I probably was.

I heard a couple of roars, but they weren't too threatening. They were all in their enclosures, keeping warm in the cold December night.

I headed for Betty's enclosure. I slipped my key into the lock as quietly as I could. I didn't want to wake her, but she was a light sleeper. She was lying on her side when I approached. Her eyes opened. She let out a low rumble, followed by a large breath of air.

"Hello, girl."

She didn't bother getting up. Her trunk curled into a hello. I removed my backpack and placed it next to her leg. It became my pillow, and she was my nighttime companion. We both fell asleep.

In the morning, a shaft of sunlight woke me. I rubbed the sleep from my eyes and sat up. Standing over me was Mr. Nagata.

"Going somewhere?"

I jumped up, almost tripping over Betty's leg.

"Mr. Nagata, good morning. What did you say?"

"The backpack. You going somewhere?"

My pack was draped over Betty's leg.

"Oh. Yeah." I fumbled for a minute, dreading how I was going to break the news to him. "Well, yeah. I am going somewhere."

He gave Betty a morning pat on the head. She didn't budge.

"You and Betty have become pretty close."

"Yeah," I said. "I always wanted a dog but I guess an elephant will do."

Mr. Nagata laughed then turned serious.

"By the way, Jack, I'm sorry I missed the ceremony."

"That's my fault. I should have called you, but it all happened so fast. She was there one day and gone the next. I wasn't thinking clearly."

He paused, studying me. "So, where are you going?"

I shifted uncomfortably, hesitating to tell him my plans. I didn't want to disappoint this man who had meant so much to me.

"After my mother passed," I told him, "I knew there was something I had to do."

"I understand," he said.

I grabbed my pack.

"I have to give my notice, sir. And I apologize for leaving so suddenly." I took a deep breath. The thought of telling him where I was going seemed nothing short of insane. "I have to go the Africa."

He cocked his head. "Africa? What for?"

"As I said, it's something I have to do, sir."

"Where in Africa?"

"Kenya. Nairobi, Kenya."

Mr. Nagata frowned. He went deep into thought for a moment, then said, "Do you know anything about Kenya?"

"I know it's in Africa."

"Well, that's a start. But why Kenya?"

"He used to talk a lot about Africa and that's the last place we heard from him. I have a feeling that's where he is."

Mr. Nagata's eyes narrowed. He looked at me like he was trying to read my mind.

"I've been to Nairobi, Jack. It's no place for a small-town kid like you."

"I'm not a kid anymore, sir."

"You know, when your father worked for me, he talked a lot about wanting to travel the world, go on an adventure." He paused as if searching for the right thing to say. "It never occurred to me he would actually do it."

Betty struggled to her feet. I stroked her trunk.

I said, "When it became obvious he wasn't coming back, it broke my mother's heart."

Mr. Nagata laid his hand on my shoulder. "I'm sorry, Jack."

It was breakfast time for Betty. She snorted which meant she was hungry. Mr. Nagata found a bucket of cabbage and handed it to me. Cabbage was to Betty like caviar is to humans. She finished the whole bucket in no time.

"Okay, if you're intent on going to Africa, there are things you need to know. There are places there that are wild and dangerous. Don't get me wrong. Africa's a wonderful, beautiful country. Magnificent mornings. Sunsets poets live for. And some of the best people in the world. But, like I said, it can be dangerous. So, if you're set on doing this, just be careful."

Betty finished her breakfast and wrapped her trunk around my arm. Although I appreciated Mr. Nagata's concern for me, it didn't change my mind.

I said to him, "Did you know elephants experience the same emotions as people? They're probably smarter than we are. They know a lot more than we think they do."

Mr. Nagata gave me a pat on the shoulder. "Come to my office before you finish up here. I have something you're going to need."

After he left, I turned to Betty. "Gotta go girl." She flapped her ears, wagged her tail. "I love you too," I told her.

When I entered Mr. Nagata's office, he was fishing around in his safe.

"I'll be with you in a minute, Jack."

He removed a large bag. Reached in and came out with a fistful of cash. He counted out a number of bills and handed them to me.

"Here's your pay and then some," he said.

"Mr. Nagata, this is too much."

"You're gonna need it."

"I don't know how I'll ever repay you."

"It's not a loan, Jack. Just make sure you come back alive."

I felt uncomfortable stuffing all that money in my pack.

"When you get to Nairobi," he said, "the first place you want to go is the Norfolk hotel."

"That's where my father's last letter was from."

"It's the most famous hotel in Nairobi. Hemingway stayed there. Make sure you meet up with an old friend of mine. His name is Phillip Cole. He used to have an office at the Norfolk. And if your father's in Nairobi, Phillip will know where to find him. Just tell him Kaito Nagata sent you." He paused a minute. "Better yet, he'll remember me by another name." He shook his head and laughed. "Just tell him Blinky sent you."

"Blinky?" I couldn't help but laugh. I gave him a what-the-hell look.

"Don't ask," he said. "Just make sure you find Phillip when you get to Nairobi," he added. "He'll help you find your father and he might even give you a job."

When we passed by the elephant enclosure, Betty was out in the yard by the fence. I stopped to say goodbye. She stuck her trunk out. I stroked her. She wiggled her ears and nuzzled me with her trunk.

"You take care of yourself, girl. I'm gonna miss you most of all."

Mr. Nagata walked me to the exit. He shook my hand.

"So, Jack," he said, "what do you plan to do when you find your father?"

"Make him pay."

"For what?"

"For breaking my mother's heart."

When I left the zoo, the last sound I heard was Betty's shrill, piercing trumpet.

7.

AFRICA 1952

WHEN I STEPPED OFF the boat at the Port of Mombasa, the first thing that hit me was the smell. I was bone tired from forty days working as a dishwasher in the stench of a galley on a tramp steamer. When I left that tin can and stepped on African soil, a westerly breeze mixed with garbage, gasoline fumes, the salty air of the Indian Ocean and the scent of spices overwhelmed me. But after a 9000-mile voyage in a ship's cramped quarters with 30 stinking crew members, Mombasa smelled like heaven.

I was told to find the ship's paymaster to pick up my wages. He had set up a makeshift table on the dock near the steamer. A crowd of angry men surrounded him, screaming and yelling. It was the crew lined up to receive their pay. The captain was nowhere to be seen. He'd been drunk most of the time aboard ship, so he was probably in some bar avoiding the crew of misfits and criminals who were now threatening the paymaster for their wages. It turned out the steamer company was charging room and board against our earnings. Nothing any of us had agreed to. The crew were getting short pay for sleeping in narrow bunks and eating prison-like food. One giant of a man who was a coal shoveler leaned over the table and grabbed the paymaster by the throat. He swore to kill him if he didn't get his money. The paymaster told him, "You'll take what we give ya and like it." Somebody wasn't gonna survive the day unless something was done and fast. It was time for cooler minds to step in.

I pushed through the crowd.

"Everybody listen up," I shouted. They ignored me. I shoved my way to the paymaster's table. "Hey, listen to me."

My bunkmate, Oklahoma, gave me a look. He shouted back, "Shut up, Jack." I don't think he was really from Oklahoma.

I raised my arms and gave it all I had. "Dammit, everyone. Shut the up and listen."

To my surprise, they all stopped and gave me their undivided attention. The coal shoveler still had the paymaster hanging by the throat.

I lowered my voice and told them, "I know you men deserve your rightful pay. But rather than do harm to this man who's just doing his job why don't you take what's yours and let him alone?"

"The kid's right," said a deckhand. "It's our money and we have a right to take what's ours."

The Captain's Chief Mate spoke up. "That would be stealing."

I thought of something a character said in a famous adventure novel that fit the moment. There's a lot of wise stuff in adventure novels.

I shouted, "It ain't stealing if you need it." I didn't exactly agree with that but I figured if it would save the paymaster's life, it was justified.

The Chief Mate came back at me. "That's stupid. Stealin' is stealin'. Ain't no two ways about it."

He had a point. But if the paymaster was going to get through the day alive, I needed to come up with a higher authority than myself. "Don't believe me," I told them. "Like I said, it ain't stealin' if you need it. And that came from none other than Mark Twain himself in a book he wrote called Huckleberry Finn."

By the slack jaws and knitted brows, you could tell they hadn't read a lot of books.

"Who the hell is Mark Twain?" Oklahoma shouted.

Maybe he was from Oklahoma.

I ignored him. "After we spent a lousy forty days pushing that sardine can halfway across the world, what we have here is not stealing. It's based on need. And we need our pay."

Twain's words reached right into their simple minds and grabbed them by their wallets.

"Yeah," shouted the big guy, "sometimes, uh, stealin' is..." He seemed confused. "Uh, sometimes..." He turned to me. "What was that you said?"

"It's not stealing if it's something you need."

The big one shouted, "He's right. We ain't stealin' nothin'. It's our pay and we need our pay."

The others chimed in. "Yeah. We need our pay, we need our pay."

A dozen men grabbed fistfuls of cash. The big fellow dropped the paymaster on the ground and claimed his share. It only took a few minutes before the money was gone along with the entire crew. I got caught up in the rush and knocked on my ass. By the time I got on my feet, the self-paid crew was long gone, and I was facing an angry paymaster flanked by two goons with billy clubs. I brushed myself off, looked the paymaster in his beady little eyes and shrugged.

"Well," I said, speaking to three fighting mad faces. "You know what they say. A friend in need is a friend indeed. And these guys were really in need."

The waters of the Indian Ocean are warm with a beautiful turquoise color. Not so in the Port of Mombasa. The sea is covered in oil slicks and garbage from all the ships docking there. The last thing anyone wants is to take a dive in those polluted waters. But the choice wasn't mine. It was my unfortunate punishment for inciting the crew to the violent overthrow of the paymaster's authority. And taking their money. When his goons tossed me into the ocean, I was lucky enough to avoid hitting my head on anything solid. I treaded water until the paymaster and his gorillas disappeared. Once on land, I headed in the direction I thought would take me to town. But now I carried with me a new smell.

I remembered Mr. Nagata's advice. He told me when I got to Mombasa, go immediately to the train station. Get a ticket to Nairobi and don't talk to anyone until you get to there.

I had walked about a mile when a bus came by and stopped. The driver asked me where I was going. He was an African with a British accent. I told him to the train station. He motioned for me to get in. He held out his hand. I dug into my pack, came up with a dollar. He shook his head. I added another dollar. He shook his head again. I took the two dollars and gave him a five. He took it and smiled. He had no teeth. I took a seat near the back. The bus was packed with locals. I was the only Westerner on board.

We lurched forward on a two-hour journey through crowded streets lined with ancient crumbling buildings, narrow garbage-filled alleys and the same sweet smell of spice that hit me when I got off the boat. We stopped a dozen times before we reached a busy section of town where the odor of spices was strong.

The bus came to a halt. Everyone on board, including the driver, quickly got off, disappearing into the passing crowds. I sat for a while not knowing what to do. Across the street was a market lined with baskets of food. I lowered the window. A rich scent swept over me.

I was out the door wandering through a market surrounded by mouth-watering baskets of spices, fruits, vegetables I'd never seen, a dozen varieties of dates, sun-tried meats, bread that looked like a Mexican tortilla. I hadn't eaten all day. I grabbed a fistful of food, paid the merchant, and headed back to the bus. I was about to board my ride when a man and woman, obviously Westerners, saw me and started laughing. I guess I looked ridiculous with an arm full of food.

"Where are you going there, sport?"

The man had a British accent. Well-dressed with the look of money.

"Just getting on my bus," I said, holding my lunch to my chest.

"Where are you headed?"

"The train station."

"Well, if you plan to get there today on that bus you're out of luck."

"Why?"

The man glanced at the woman. I couldn't hear what he said to her. Whatever he said caused them both to laugh. He turned to me.

"Where you from?"

"United States."

"Well, sport, if you're waiting for the driver, odds are he won't be coming back any time today."

"Where'd he go?" I scanned the crowd as if I could spot the driver.

"Home. A bar. Who knows where these people go? You can't count on them. If you must get to the train station soon, it won't be on that bus."

The woman he was with was strikingly beautiful. She smiled and winked at me. The man held out his hand.

"Hello, chap. I'm David Newman and this is my wife, Kate."

I held out my free hand still clutching my lunch in the other arm. I nodded to his wife.

"And you are?" he asked.

"I'm Jack."

"Jack...?"

"Jack Quill."

David's brow pushed his eyes into a squint. He traded strange glances with his wife.

"Did you say Quill?"

"Yeah."

He shifted uncomfortably. Looked around as if expecting someone else.

"So, Jack Quill. Are you alone?"

"Yeah," I said.

"What brings you to Africa?"

"I'm looking for my father."

His eyes narrowed. The question came out pinched, nervous. "What's your father's name?"

"J.A. J.A. Quill."

David stiffened, rocked back on his heels. His face tensed. Kate moved behind him, peering at me over his shoulder. David's cool attitude turned sour.

"You are J.A. Quill's son?"

I nodded. "Yeah. Do you know him?"

David swallowed hard. He glared at me.

"Would you like a ride to the train station?"

I shrugged. "Sure."

8.

DAVID'S WHITE FORD CONVERTIBLE wound through a maze of narrow streets barely wide enough for two cars. At times, a crush of people jammed the streets, slowing us down. David honked his horn, yelling at them to move aside. Kate, his wife, tried to calm him, but David's anger seemed to be about more than people in a crowded street.

After what seemed like hours pushing through sweltering heat and too many back streets, David stopped the Ford in an alley. Kate gave him a quick kiss and got out.

"Make the call," he said to her.

She nodded. A hurried glance at me. She went into a building.

I said, "Where are we?"

David hit the gas and shot down a side street.

"How far is the train station?" I shouted.

David wasn't answering. I held on for dear life, swaying as he wheeled the car left and right. My lunch spilled on the floor. We finally came to a screeching stop in another tight alley. He jumped out of the car and faced me.

"Okay, get out."

This was definitely not the train station.

"What the hell's going on?"

He pulled out a pistol and pointed it at me.

"Move," he said. "Now."

I had the feeling I was going to miss my train.

David forced me into a small apartment where a man sat on a living room couch. Another man stood nearby. The man on the couch was dressed in an expensive suit, smoking a cigarette in a holder. I'd only seen that in movies. The other man was over six feet tall. He had gray steely eyes that darted around like he was scanning for enemies. He stood rigid, his fists doubled at his sides.

The man on the couch stood up.

"Hello, old chap. My name is Walter." His accent was obviously British.

Walter extended his hand. I noticed the fingernails trimmed and polished. They were hands that had never seen manual work. When I ignored him, he withdrew. He took the cigarette holder between his thumb and forefinger and held it away from him, like a lady would. He studied me for a moment.

"So, you are the son of the great J.A. Quill," he said.

"Yeah, but I don't know what you mean about him being great," I said.

David stood by the door, gun still in hand.

I asked Walter, "Do you know my father?"

"Yes, I do. And your name is Jack, right?"

"Yeah."

Walter pointed at David. "You have already been introduced to my partner, David. And this is my associate, Jake." Walter grinned. "Jake and Jack. I think you two are going to get along famously."

I glanced at Jake. He was built like a linebacker and looked like he wanted to tackle me. I did not want to have anything to do with this guy, much less famously.

Walter motioned to a chair opposite the couch.

"Please have a seat, Jack."

"What is this all about?" I asked, refusing to sit.

Walter said, "If you'll please have a seat, I'd be glad to explain."

I glanced at David. The pistol was still in his hand. Walter noticed.

"You can put the gun away, David. We won't be needing that."

David stuck the pistol in his jacket. Walter turned to me.

"I have only one question to ask you. Give me the answer I want and you can be on your way." Walter came face to face with me. "Where's your father?"

"Why do you wanna know?"

"We have business with him," he said. He flicked the ashes of his cigarette into his hand then deposited the ashes in a nearby ashtray. "All I want to know is where we can find J.A. Quill." He gave me a sideways look. "You do know where he is, don't you?"

"As a matter of fact, I don't."

Walter bowed his head and gave me a funny look. "You don't expect us to believe that do you?"

"Believe it or not, it's true. And even if I knew, I wouldn't tell you."

Walter smacked his lips, shook his head. "Oh, Jack, that is not a good answer." He turned to Jake and nodded. Jake came straight at me so fast I didn't have time to react. He slammed his fist into my jaw, sending me crashing into the chair.

"What the hell was that for?" I said, nursing my jaw.

Walter's civilized act turned sour. He got in my face, the tip of his cigarette threatening to burn my nose.

"I won't ask you again," he said.

"You can ask me all day but my answer is still the same. I don't know where my father is." I shook off the stars swimming in my head. "Anyway, what is so important about finding my father?"

Walter clenched the cigarette holder in his teeth. It bounced as he spoke. "He owes us a lot of money and we want it back."

"I swear, I really don't know where he is," I said. "I just got here."

"What do you mean you just got here?" Walter asked.

"I just got off a boat a few hours ago. I haven't had time to find him."

Walter blinked. "Well, he must have told you where to find him when you got here. I can't imagine a father not telling a son where he is after you travelled from God knows where."

"From Virginia," I said. "It's in the United States."

"And you haven't talked to him since you got here?"

I shook my head. "I haven't spoken to him in eleven years."

Walter frowned, started pacing. He took a long drag on his cigarette. He wheeled around.

"If you don't know where he is, why did you come to Kenya?"

"His last letter was from Kenya," I said. "It seemed the best place to start looking for him."

"I think you're lying," he said. "I think you know exactly where he is and you're protecting him."

My voice went ballistic. "I'm not lying. I don't know where the son-of-a-bitch is and I'm the last person who wants to protect him."

Walter rested an elbow on his chest and cradled his chin in his hand. Again, studying me. "You seem like a nice kid. Not at all like your father."

"I wouldn't know what he's like now."

Walter folded his arms. He looked at David. "What are we going to do with this young man?"

David was totally pissed off. "Let's hold the little shit for ransom."

Walter shook his head so hard I thought the cigarette holder was going to fly out of his mouth.

"No, no, no. I may not like J.A. Quill, but to hold his son ransom is a sure death sentence." Walter punched his next words like he was in a boxing match. "You don't cross J.A. Quill and live to tell about it."

I shook my head. "My father might be a lot of things but he's not a killer."

Walter and David looked at each other in disbelief.

"You don't know what business your father's in, do you?" Walter said.

I was getting tired of the questions. I had a train to catch. "The last I heard from him he was in Africa on safari."

They broke out laughing. Jake joined in.

Walter said to me, "Safari, huh? Well, I guess that's one way of putting it."

I needed to get out of there. There was no way past that mountain of a man guarding the door. Walter seemed to be chewing on a thought. His cigarette was down to its last ash. He took the stub between two fingers and dumped it in the ashtray. He put the holder in the inside pocket of his jacket. Checked his watch. It looked expensive.

"Kid, I have to be going. Please accept my apologies for putting you through all of this. For what it's worth, I believe you don't know where your father is. Anyone who would travel halfway around the world to find someone without knowing where they are…" He made a tsk, tsk sound. "Well, anyone that stupid has got to be telling the truth." He turned to go but stopped to say one last thing. "And please, when you see your father, don't tell him what happened here. Just let him know I would like to have a civilized meeting with him to discuss…" Walter closed his eyes and took a deep breath. "He'll know."

He motioned to David and Jake to follow and then they left.

There went my ride to the train station.

9.

THE MOMBASA TO NAIROBI express was scheduled to arrive at 7 p.m. I got to the station a little after 5 p.m. There was a long line waiting to buy tickets. By the time I got to the ticket window, the clerk told me there were no more second-class tickets. Only first-class. I paid up and headed for the platform.

The Mombasa Railway Station was a large, pitched-roof structure covered by a long shed over the platform. The platform swarmed with native travelers waiting for the ride to Nairobi. I later learned the crowds were made of up Maasai, Kikuyu, Arabs and, of course, the English. If the physical features of the crowd didn't reveal their tribes, the clothing did.

White robes and turbans marked Arab travelers. The Maasai believed their bright multi-colored shukas scared lions away. The Kikuyu wore square pieces of red and blue cloth draped over their bodies. Then there were the British. Bush jackets, terai hats, khaki jodhpurs, and pith helmets. The mob of people chattering in a dozen different languages and dialects, milling about waiting on a long train trip made me want to fly to Nairobi. But that would cost me all the money I had. The train it was.

I moved beyond the crush of bodies to the west side of the platform. When I broke through the crowd, the horror I saw stopped me cold.

A team of men struggled to unload what appeared to be large white objects from railroad cars lined up on sidings. The workers were East Indians dressed only in turbans and short white loincloths. At first, I didn't realize what they were unloading. I think my mind was so shocked at the nature of the cargo it took a minute to accept what was happening.

The mountain of large, white objects were elephant tusks. Ivory. Tons of it.

My first thought was of Betty. My beautiful elephant friend Betty who liked apples and whose touch with that magnificent trunk was as gentle as a feather. Betty, safely at the Virginia zoo. The thought of someone, some monstrous person, killing her and cutting off her tusks sickened me.

I stared at the stack of ivory. My stomach churned at the thought of the carnage it took to slaughter enough elephants to produce the heap of tusks scorching in the sun.

The mound of tusks covered an area twice as tall as a man and ten times wider. A group of men stood to one side waving pieces of paper, shouting and arguing with a frumpy-looking guy who appeared to be conducting a sale. The frumpy guy wore a funny-looking hat I'd never seen before. I later learned it was called a slouch hat.

I walked over to the huddle and pushed my way to the front. The frumpy guy turned to me.

"Who the hell are you?"

He wasn't an Englishman.

I tried to sound official. "What's going on here?" I asked.

The group went silent, staring at me.

"Aye don't know who you are, mate, but this is a private auction."

Turned out Mr. Frumpy was from Australia. My anger got the best of me. I went toe to toe with him. He was a solid five and a half feet tall and almost as wide. At six-two, I towered over him. He stood his ground. I took stock of the buyers in this depraved negotiation. A crew of misfits, degenerates, and bottom feeders.

I pointed to the ivory mountain.

"That ivory came from magnificent living creatures. And you murdered them and cut their body parts off for money? What kind of depraved asshole are you?"

"I ain't murdered nobody, mate."

"You might as well have. You're dealing in murder. All of you butchers."

"Get outta me face, kid, or I'll have a go atcha."

"You'll have a go at me? Then I'll report you to the authorities and you'll end up spending your miserable life in prison."

The Aussie threw his head back, laughing.

"The authorities? Hell, you little dickhead, I am the authority."

I took a swing at his square jaw and connected. It was like hitting a tank. To my surprise, he didn't fall. A trickle of blood dropped from his nose. He shook his head and blinked. "Well, shoot me dead."

He lunged at me. Barreled his head into my chest. We fell to the ground. The buyers scurried out of the way. The Aussie bear-hugged me. Almost crushed my ribcage. I clapped hands over his ears and he screamed, letting go his grip. I jumped up, got on top of him, pounding my fists into his face. I got in a few good licks before something hit me in the head. I blacked out.

I remember being dragged a long way. Dropped into a dark place. Then oblivion.

I woke later to a bright light hanging above my head. The glare was blinding. I was sitting in a folding chair in a small room without windows. I panicked. Looked around for my pack. It was under my chair.

A door opened. Bright sunlight flooded the room. I squinted, throwing up a hand to block out the sun. The door closed. Hovering over me were two uniformed African men. I guessed they were policemen.

"I am Officer Amel, head of security," the tall one said. "Do you know why we brought you here?"

"No," I said.

"You are being charged with assault and battery of an auctioneer. Do you remember attacking one Charles Bowman?"

My head cleared.

"I don't know who that is."

"Mr. Bowman is a respected auctioneer in Mombasa. As he reported, he was conducting a legal auction when you, without provocation, attacked him. Do you remember the attack?"

I nodded. "Yeah, and I would do it again. The man's a murderer."

"I beg your pardon?"

"He was selling elephant body parts."

"Sir, he was auctioning ivory. The selling of ivory is a legal enterprise in Mombasa, and Mr. Bowman was just doing his job when you assaulted him." The Officer took a deep breath. "Unfortunately for you, Mr. Bowman has pressed charges."

"Am I under arrest?" I asked.

"Yes, and I'm afraid we will have to detain you until you go before a magistrate."

"What's a magistrate?"

"You are an American, aren't you, sir?"

I nodded.

"It's what you call a judge."

I was starting to worry. "Am I going to jail?"

"That is up to the magistrate. Assault is a very serious matter here, sir. I doubt you will be going home very soon."

I swallowed hard. "Look, I'm sorry. When I saw all that ivory I..."

He cut me off. He was getting testy.

"What is your name, sir?"

"Jack. Jack Quill."

Officer Amel and his assistant looked at each other.

"Did you say Quill?"

"Yes."

The Officer frowned. He gave me a look I didn't like.

"May I see some identification?"

I reached under the chair for my pack. I found my passport and handed it to the Officer. He flipped through it. Handed it to me.

"What is your business here in Mombasa, Mr. Quill?"

"I don't have any business here. I'm headed for Nairobi."

The Officer studied me. "Quill. That's an unusual name."

I shrugged. "Not in my family."

"How long have you been in Mombasa?"

"I just got here today."

"Do you have family here in Kenya?"

"I think my father is in Nairobi."

Officer Amel hesitated. He shifted nervously.

"What is your father's name?"

"Jonathan Allen Quill. He goes by J.A. Quill."

The Officer and his assistant exchanged worried glances. He gave me a sideways look.

"Your father is J.A. Quill?"

"Yes," I said. "Do you know him?"

He blinked several times.

"Excuse us."

He and his assistant left in a hurry.

I felt the back of my head. A sharp pain. An egg-sized knot. Whoever hit me must have used a baseball bat.

It wasn't long before the Officer and his assistant returned. They were nervous. Officer Amel wiped his brow with a handkerchief. He glanced at me again.

"You said you have just arrived in Mombasa. Correct?"

"Yes," I said, losing my patience.

"And you are headed to Nairobi?"

"I told you that already," I said.

"And what is your purpose in Nairobi?"

"To find my father."

The Officer looked surprised. "You don't know where he is?"

My voice went up an octave. "I just got the shit kicked out of me by a couple of guys asking questions about where my father is. What's going on here?"

"What guys?"

"Walter, David and Jake somebody."

The Officer turned to his assistant. "I'll handle this."

The assistant left the room. The officer faced me.

"This Walter person. What did he look like?"

I thought for a minute. "Suit and tie. Smoked a cigarette in a holder. He was what we call a dandy back in the States."

The Officer went pale. He didn't look happy.

"I see," he said. He gave me a phony smile. "Would you please excuse me?"

He left in a hurry.

More waiting. My headache was having headaches. I tried to put together all that had happened since I got to Africa. The trouble with David and Walter. The fight with the Aussie. Now, these threats from the Officer. Nothing was making sense.

Finally, the Officer returned.

"Mister Quill, I want to apologize for any inconvenience we've caused you. It appears Mr. Bowman has misrepresented the altercation he had with you. He confessed he instigated the entire episode. He has asked that you accept his apology."

"He's apologizing for me hitting him? I don't understand."

"He has refused to press charges. You are free to go."

I threw up my hands. "First, you tell me I'm arrested for hitting this auctioneer guy. And how I've got to go before a judge who's probably gonna throw me in jail. Then when I tell you who my father is, I get apologies and I'm free to go? What is it about my father in this damned country that people seem to be afraid of?"

"Are you booked on today's express to Nairobi?"

"Yes."

He looked at his watch.

"It is due to arrive in about forty-five minutes. Passengers are already lining up to board. I suggest you take your kit and get to the platform. And Mombasa wants to extend its best wishes for your stay in our country."

He gave me a sharp look.

I said, "You obviously know who my father is. Do you know where I can find him?"

"Please, sir. You must go now."

He hurried out the door.

10.

THERE WAS A WILD rush for the trains. The boarding frenzy started before the locomotive came to a screeching halt. Clouds of steam from the engines filled the platform. People raced through the smoke like escapees from hell headed toward the third-class railway cars.

The first-class cars were at the back of the train. I watched as groups of well-dressed passengers strolled elegantly toward the privileged upper-class transportation. Women in fashionable white dresses and lacey hats, arms linked to their gentlemen decked out in pressed white pants, buttoned vests and pith helmets. And me, reeking of Indian ocean garbage, oil slick, dirty jeans, stained shirt, a torn jacket holding a first-class ticket. I was certainly not fit for first-class. I thought I might try to join the multitudes in third-class when a portly gentleman sporting a mustache said to me with a proper English accent, "I say there, boy, are you lost?"

He wore the traditional getup of a white hunter. Jodhpurs, a khaki vest, a satin ascot and a pith helmet. Tucked under his arm was a well-worn but expensive looking leather rifle case.

"No, sir. I'm just trying to decide where I should go."

He noticed the ticket in my hand.

"Is that a first-class ticket?"

"Yes, sir."

"Then you belong with us." He looked me up and down. "Good God, man. Where the bloody hell have you been?"

I shoved my hands in my jacket.

"Sorry, I know I'm not dressed for travel. I just got off the boat."

"You look like you just got off a tramper?"

His moustache slanted into a sneer.

"Sir," I said, "I think maybe I got the wrong ticket. Maybe I belong..." I nodded toward the third- class cars.

The Englishman huffed.

"Are you daft? You're a white man. White men don't mix with their kind." He examined me again, stroking that bush under his nose. "Now, we've got to do something about your clothes." He took a deep whiff. "Good Lord, you smell as bad as boiled cabbage. Where have you been?"

"I'm somewhat of an adventurer. And us adventurers don't always have access to modern conveniences."

"Well, if you're going to socialize with polite society, you must conform to accepted standards of cleanliness."

A shrill whistle got our attention. The English gentleman grabbed my arm.

"Time to board, young man. We'll do something about that..." He made a circular motion with his finger pointed at my clothes. "About that later."

A uniformed man stepped off the train and yelled, "Stand away!" Bystanders stepped back from the train. The uniformed man blew the whistle again.

"Forgive me, Chap." The Englishman held out his hand. "I'm Harry Dankworth." We shook hands. He said, "And you are?"

"Jack."

He let go of my hand. Stared down his nose. "Just Jack?"

After all the trouble I'd been through using my real name, I decided it was time to borrow my mother's maiden name.

"Jack Sims."

"You're American, aren't you?"

"Yes, sir."

"I met some jolly good mates in the war from America. Always glad to help a Yank."

"Thank you, sir."

He gave me a sideways glance.

"But you are one smelly Yank."

He laughed as he waddled off toward the upper crust.

"We'll have to do something about that."

11.

THE FIRST-CLASS PASSENGER CAR was a showcase of class and money. Fashionable women, well-dressed men parading through the narrow coach, heading toward their compartments. Harry stopped at a cubicle at the front of the car. He told me to leave my pack on one of the seats. We proceeded down the crowded passageway, squeezing past ladies smelling of perfume and men's trailing scent of spicy aftershave. Some women wore safari gear. Hard to imagine these delicate-looking creatures sporting a rifle aimed at a charging lion. A lot of the men wore field gear. I noticed a few rifle cases in overhead bins.

Running the gauntlet of that pompous group, I knew my stench was strong enough to draw attention. There were some sneers, heads turned, frowns, and ladies covering their noses with lacy handkerchiefs. I couldn't blame them. I smelled as bad as I looked.

I followed Harry through two luxury coaches. Everyone seemed to know him. Women touched him as he passed, calling him by name. He answered with a grunt or a nod.

The third car was a formal dining area. Tables set with polished silverware, crystal glasses, starched white tablecloths. The chairs were soft leather. Walls gleamed with polished wood. Very inviting. I was hungry, but that would have to wait.

We finally reached the kitchen. I heard a crash of metal, curses. We entered to find three African cooks arguing with each other. As soon as Harry appeared, they came to attention. The head cook saluted and said something in a language I didn't understand.

"What did he say?" I asked.

Harry waved his arms, shouting in the same language I later learned was Swahili. The cooks bowed their heads as Harry obviously chewed them out about something. He turned to me.

"You stay here for a while. And don't talk to them."

He turned to go.

"Why am I staying here?"

"You'll find out very soon."

Harry left. A train whistle blew. We were underway.

The cooks immediately relaxed. The head cook came over to me.

"Hello. I am Azaan. My friends call me Azi."

He wiped his hands on his apron.

I nodded. "Hi." I flipped a thumb at the door. "What was that all about?"

Azi shrugged. He gave me a wide grin, nodding. "Who knows?" He looked at the other two cooks. "That's Hasani and George."

"George?"

They broke out laughing.

"His real name is Rafiki, but he didn't like it. He wanted an English name so he chose the King, King George."

I nodded toward George.

"Your majesty."

That killed them. I thought Rafiki-George was going to fall on the floor laughing.

"And what is your name?" Azi asked.

"Jack."

"Jack. You are American."

"Right."

"Okay, American Jack. Are you hungry?"

"Yeah. You got any hamburgers and french fries?"

"Only English food." Hasani said, "The English don't like American food."

George bent over a sink, washing dishes. He chuckled. "They don't like Americans."

Hasani chimed in. "They don't even like us. And this is our country."

"So, what do you have for breakfast? Any donuts?"

Azi shook his head. "No donuts. But we've got scones."

"What's a scone?" I asked.

"It's like a sweet biscuit."

"You got any coffee?"

Azi turned to Hasani. "Coffee for the boss. And a scone." He pointed at a small table and chair. "Please, American Jack, sit."

I sat at the chair waiting for breakfast.

Hasani opened a container and took out a scone. It looked like a biscuit. Hasani grabbed a cup and poured coffee. He put the scone on a plate with a small knife and beside it something like jam. Handed it to me watching as I stared at the scone.

"Thank you," I said.

"You're welcome, boss."

I examined the scone. Smeared it with jam. Took a sip of coffee and a bite of the scone. "Wow, this is good. Did you make this, Hasani?"

"Yes, boss."

"Why are you calling me boss?"

Azi said, "You're a white man. All white men are think they're boss."

I shook my head. "I'm nobody's boss. Just call me Jack."

They all glanced at each other and smiled. Azi said, "Okay, boss."

I drank my coffee and ate the scone while the three cooks continued working.

"So, what's for dinner?" I asked.

Azi said, "English dinner. Roast meat, potatoes, yorkshire pudding, and carrot soup."

"So, where'd you learn to cook, Azi?"

"Detroit," he said.

I almost choked on my coffee. "Detroit? You mean like United States Detroit?"

"Yes," he said.

"When were you in Detroit?"

"Not long ago."

"Why Detroit?"

"I have a cousin there."

"How did you like it?"

"I was only there a few months. I got homesick." He went silent. A mood came over him.

"You didn't like America?"

He shook his head.

"America did not like me."

The train lurched. Steam drifted by a small window above my table. The three cooks settled into their jobs. Azi busied himself cutting potatoes on a hardboard.

"Hey, Azi."

He looked at me.

"I don't care what America likes. I like you."

A faint smile of thanks. I finished my coffee and asked if I could help. They all shook their heads. I leaned back in my chair and dozed off dreaming of hamburgers and french fries. And a cold Coca Cola.

12.

I fell.

ACTUALLY, HARRY KICKED MY chair out from under me. I hit the floor hard. Harry stood over me, mouth pursed, eyes narrowed, staring at me. To his left and right, a slender fellow and another chubby guy like Harry. All three dressed in safari outfits glaring at me like I was a cockroach they were about to crush.

"Get up, boy," Harry said.

I struggled. Caught a foot in the chair. Shoved it aside. Pushed up on my feet. Harry's friends gave me the once over. The tall one spoke.

"So, this is the Yank you told us about."

The chubby one put the back of his hand to his nose.

"You were right, Harry. He smells like elephant piss."

I turned to chubby.

"Who the hell are you?"

Harry pointed a thumb at chubby.

"This is Arthur. And this gentleman..." He nodded to the slim one next to him. "This is Sir Wallace Hemmings."

"Could you people tell me what's going on?" I asked.

The one called Arthur stroked his moustache. All three of them had moustaches.

"Well, young man, it's your appearance," Arthur said. "And your bodily odor. I'm afraid we cannot allow you to continue in first-class in your present condition. These are all friends and acquaintances of ours and frankly they are unaccustomed to mingling with, how should I put it, low standards of hygiene."

The three cooks were busy with dinner. They clearly wanted no part of this. I didn't even know what this was yet.

"What do you mean I can't socialize with people in first-class?" I turned to Harry. "Harry, you're the one who said I couldn't ride in third-class because I'm a white man. I remind you I have a first-class ticket. So, are you people telling me there are different classes of white men?"

Sir What's-His-Name twirled his moustache. These guys had a thing about playing with their moustaches.

"Actually, there are different classes of white men," Sir-What's-His-Name said. "Mainly, rich white men and the poor."

Harry added, "And the educated."

All three guffawed. English gentlemen never laughed, they guffawed. Sounded like laughing and choking at the same time.

"So," Arthur chimed in, "which are you, young man? Rich, poor, educated or not?"

"I'm an American and that outranks all of you snobby assholes."

That didn't go over well.

Harry said, "Frankly, Jack, we've already had too many complaints about your befoulment. And since dinner will be served in half an hour, you simply cannot be seated in your condition."

"What do I do? There's no place here to take a shower."

Harry and company exchanged glances. "I think we have a solution," he said.

I got the feeling something was about to happen I didn't want to happen. I thought of all the adventure heroes in the many books I grew up reading. I thought of myself as an adventurer, like them. Not as some kid whose parents were about to force him to take his Saturday bath. Whatever these men had planned for me was based on their misunderstanding of who I was. I had to correct their misconception before they did something crazy.

"Gentlemen," I started, "while I can appreciate your concern as to my present condition, and I do apologize for offending any of you or your friends, but, you see, I'm an adventurer. And as you know, the life of an adventurer subjects him to circumstances that are not always civilized. While I do apologize for my present state, I would like the respect any globetrotter like myself is entitled to. I ask you if Jim Hawkins of *Treasure Island* stood before you in his primitive offensiveness, or Robinson Crusoe, whose years on a desert island probably rendered him repulsive, or Allan Quartermain, who searched unexplored regions of Africa without a decent change of clothes. If they stood before you as I do, would you judge their unfortunate appearance harshly considering the horrendous experiences they had suffered?"

In the silence that followed, I realized the train had stopped.

They dragged me kicking and screaming outside. I faced a party of men and servants carrying buckets of water, clothing, and towels. The sun had fallen below the horizon, leaving an illuminated sky.

We headed for a rundown train station with the name Mariakani painted on a dilapidated building. I assumed it was the name of a town. They lifted me airborne on the arms of half a dozen brutes. I was carried to the rear of the station where they dumped me on the ground like so much garbage. Harry and Sir-What's-His-Name picked me up and stood me on my feet. A circle of determined men surrounded me.

Harry stepped forward.

"All right," he said. "Disrobe."

"You mean as in naked?"

Harry, Arthur, and Sir-What's-His-Name nodded. I got the impression they were enjoying this on some level I didn't understand. I defiantly shoved my hands in my pockets. Smiled. Looking for a hint of a joke. Nothing. Dead serious scowls.

"Is this some king of initiation?"

Harry said, "You might call it that."

"Like welcoming me into a club?"

"Stop stalling, mate," Arthur said.

"So, what's the name of this club?" I asked.

"It's called..." Harry turned to his cohorts. The guffaws scared a flock of birds away. Harry turned to me.

"It's called initiating you into proper English society."

"You're kidding."

They weren't.

"To hell with you people. I'm not doing it."

Harry got nose to nose with me.

"Fine with me, bloke. But if you don't, you don't get back on the train."

"You're bluffing."

They weren't.

I never had my clothes ripped off by a bunch of guys. There was a girl once. But that's another story.

Clothes off. Someone shoved a bar of soap at me. I surrendered to my fate. Started scrubbing weeks of grim away. Bath in the company of strangers. Drowned me in buckets of water. A towel thrown at me. Dried off as quick as I could. A stack of clothes and a pair of boots. Some of the fellows turned away as I dressed. A strange courtesy since they'd already seen me naked. Jolly considerate of them. I put on a pair of safari pants, shirt, tugged at the boots that didn't fit. I threw them aside and put on my sneakers. Harry stuck a terai hat on my head. He faced his entourage.

"Gentlemen. Shall we?"

On the way to the train, Harry patted me on the back.

"Good sport, old chum."

Faces peered out of the train, wondering what mischief the group of men had engaged in. If they only knew.

I followed Harry, Arthur, and Sir-What's-His-Name into the first-class car. As we entered, passengers peered out of their compartments. A few women applauded. Men held up victory thumbs. Harry led our group to the first-class carriage and a compartment for four. Harry ceremoniously stepped aside, gesturing for me to enter. I sat by the door. Harry and company took seats across from me. The train wheels engaged. A whistle blew. On to Nairobi.

The three Englishmen decided to take a short nap. I couldn't sleep so I folded my arms and waited for their next move. An hour later, they woke up.

Harry focused on me like he was surprised I was there. Then he seemed to remember who I was.

He slapped me on the knee and said, "Well, old chap, now that you're fit for civilized society, it's time for dinner."

The four of us took our places in the dining car, seated at a classy table. The ladies and gentlemen who earlier cast critical eyes on me now accepted my improvements with gentlemanly nods and ladylike winks. Harry noticed the attention.

"We don't see many Americans these days. They're quite the novelty."

"A novelty?" I said.

Harry spoke up. "Yes, chap. Actually, attempting to civilize you reminds me of the story of Eliza Doolittle."

"Who's she?" I asked.

Sir-What's-His-Name raised eyebrows.

Servers entered the cabin carrying trays of knives, forks, spoons, plates, and glasses. They busied themselves replacing the knives, forks, spoons, plates, and glasses that were already there. I was ignorant of the ways of rich people. They sure wasted a lot of effort being rich.

The servers wore white gloves, ankle-length dresses, and strange red hats shaped like upside down bowls.

"My word, man," Harry said, continuing the conversation about this Doolittle woman. "Surely you've heard of Eliza Doolittle."

I shook my head, knowing embarrassment was lurking in my future.

"No,' I said, "I'm sorry but I don't know of Miss Doolittle."

"Have you heard of Bernard Shaw?" Sir-What's-His-Name asked.

I shook my head. "Is he related to Miss Doolittle?"

I noticed the placement of silverware. Three forks on the left. Two knives and a spoon on the right. And a few smaller utensils and plates that seemed useless. A server startled me when he laid a napkin on my lap.

"Pygmalion, man. Pygmalion."

I shrugged again. "Pig what?"

Sir-What's-His-Name threw up his hands.

"My God, you Americans are such bores."

Arthur, holding a glass of water between his thumb and index finger, shook his head. "I think it's going to take more than a bath to civilize this one."

The three of them ignored me, launching into a deep intellectual discussion about this Shaw guy. I tried to keep up, but it was beyond my knowledge.

It was at that moment I first saw her. As soon as she entered the dining car my world went silent. All conversation faded. My eyes focused on her.

She was about five and a half feet tall. Long, silky black hair. Sky-blue eyes. Perfect lips. No makeup. She wore a brown jacket, a white shirt and a tie, brown trousers with boots. By her side, a tall blond woman. Handsome in a hard way. Obviously, her protector. Maybe her mother. They entered at the far end of the dining car. They took their seats with the girl facing me, the mother's back to me. The girl's beauty so overwhelming it was impossible not to stare. And I wasn't the only one staring. Men and women were checking her out.

"Jack?"

My three companions stared at me.

Harry said, "The server is waiting."

I came out of my trance. A server in an ankle-length white robe hovered over me.

Harry spoke. "He's waiting for you to order."

I shifted in my seat. A menu on my plate. I examined it, then glanced at the girl. I nodded toward her.

"The girl at the end," I said to the server. "Do you know who she is?"

Harry, Arthur, and Sir What's-His-Name turned to look. Harry took a long look at the girl. He said, "Are you nutters? She's out of your class, Jack."

The servers started taking orders. I looked at the menu again. Just as Azi said. Roast meat, potatoes, yorkshire pudding, and carrot soup.

The server stared at me.

"I'll have it all," I said.

The server gave me a critical look.

Harry rolled his eyes and said to the server, "American."

The server nodded and left.

Harry and company launched into a conversation about hunting, totally ignoring me. The server brought tea and the carrot soup. It was a pale version of Campbell's tomato soup. We were all having the soup.

Hungry as I was, I dove in. As soon as I did, Harry cleared his throat and leveled his beady eyes on me.

"Wrong spoon," he said.

I noticed there was another bigger spoon. Harry nodded. More civilizing.

I was about to take a sip of carrot soup when I caught the girl at the end of the car staring at me. I smiled. Some soup dribbled down my chin. Forgetting myself, I wiped it away with my sleeve. She shook her head and laughed. Her mother turned around, caught me looking and glared at me with protective, motherly eyes. An idea popped into my head. I'll turn my embarrassment into a joke on myself as a way to meet her. I pushed my chair back and said to Harry and company, "Excuse me, I'll be right back."

Harry said, "Where are you going?"

"To meet someone."

With my eyes fixed on her, I stood.

I miscalculated.

I stood up too quickly, upending the table and everything on it. Glasses of water splashed everywhere. A couple of plates crashed to the floor. Beef scattered, potatoes rolled, silverware rattled. The orange soup splashed all over me, Harry, Arthur and Sir-What's-His-Name. The noise reverberated throughout the cabin. I jumped back, apologizing. Harry bolted out of his chair, almost losing his balance, his pants soaked with orange soup. Sir-Whoever backed away so the server could clean up the mess. I glanced at the girl. She obviously saw everything that had happened. She was grinning. Her mother wasn't. I gave the girl a weak, guilty smile.

I sat, head bowed, humiliated. My one shot at romance, ruined.

I looked at Harry. "How soon till we get to Nairobi?"

His face was red with anger, his jacket soup orange.

"Not soon enough."

13.

SLEEPING ON A TRAIN rocks you to sleep. The sway of the cars, the rhythm of the wheels sent me into dreamland when my head hit the pillow. The good gentlemen, Harry, Arthur, and Sir-What's-His-Name, were kind enough to allow me to bunk in their sleeping car. We got to bed a little after dinner. I was lucky enough to get the upper berth. During the night, I woke a few times to the almost unbearable snoring of my three companions. Then I went back to sleep.

I woke at first light to six eyes staring at me. They weren't friendly eyes. Harry was especially angry. I found out why when he lifted his hand. In it was the name tag he had removed from my pack. "J.A. Quill."

I grinned. "I can explain."

Being thrown off a moving train hurts. They must have convinced the engineer to slow down enough so the fall wouldn't kill me. They left me at a decrepit train station called Stony Athi. It was not really what you would call a station, just a small building of rusted tin with boarded-up windows. It made the rundown train station at Mariakani look like a king's mansion.

It was about eight in the morning. As the train pulled away, my former gentlemen companions gathered at the window, grinning as they raised their middle fingers goodbye. I had no idea how far Nairobi was. I looked around, trying to get my bearings when I saw a man standing not far away staring at me. He had on a white collar and a robe. In his hand is a black book.

"Good morning, son. Can I help you?" the man said.

Another Brit.

"I am Father Dixon. And you are…?"

"Jack," I told him

We shook hands. I wasn't a Catholic but I knew a Catholic priest when I saw one.

"It is good to meet you, Jack. You are American," he said.

I nodded.

"Are you lost?" he said.

"No, sir. I got kicked off the train. And I don't know how I'm going to get to Nairobi."

"Who did such a thing?"

"It's a long story. Do you know when the next train is?"

"Not until early tomorrow."

"How far is Nairobi?"

"About fifteen miles," he said.

"I guess I could walk."

Father Dixon laughed. "That would be very dangerous."

"Why?"

"There are lions."

"Do you have a car?" I asked.

"No," he said.

I studied the area. There was no church in sight.

"Where's your church?

"I am stationed at the Cathedral Basilica in Nairobi."

"What are you doing here?"

"Attending to the sick and the needy."

"How did you get here?" I asked.

He shrugged. "I walked."

"What about the lions? Weren't you afraid?"

He smiled, patting the book in his hand. "I have no fear. God is always with me."

"Well, I need to get to Nairobi," I said, "so, if I walk to with you, will God be with me too?"

He smiled. "If you have faith."

I had no choice. "Lead the way," I said.

We walked parallel to the railroad tracks for about a mile. The weather was hot. My pack was weighing me down. I was about to ask Father Dixon if we could rest when I saw the dust trail of a truck headed toward us on a nearby road. Father Dixon stopped and watched as the truck got close. He turned to me. I could see concern on his face.

"They are Kikuyu. Let me do the talking."

An open truck loaded with six Africans barreled toward us, coming to a skidding halt only yards away. Some had machetes. Others had guns. The one who seemed in charge had a gun. They jumped out of the truck and surrounded us.

Father Dixon held up his hands. "I am a priest, and this is my friend, Jack. We were headed to Nairobi. We want no trouble."

The leader's eyes were bloodshot, open wide, darting from me to Father Dixon.

"How do I know you are a priest?"

"I am Father Dixon. I serve at the Cathedral Basilica in Nairobi."

The leader sneered. "Many white men hide behind the church. I am not convinced."

Father Dixon raised the Bible. "I am a man of God. I go in peace."

The leader slapped Father Dixon's hand with his rifle butt, sending the Father's Bible skipping across the crushed stones lining the railroad tracks. I picked the Bible up and tried to hand it to Father Dixon. The leader grabbed the Bible from my hand and tossed it into nearby brush.

He turned on me. "Who are you?"

I tried to steady my voice. "My name is Jack and I'm not from here."

The leader turned to his circle of goons. They all laughed.

"You're American but you're just as white as he is."

"What does that have to do with anything?" I asked.

That got the biggest laugh from the gang. The leader dropped his smile and moved toward me, pushing the point of the rifle against my nose.

"It has everything to do with it," he said, turning to Father Dixon. "Right, Father?"

When Father Dixon spoke, his British accent seemed heavier. He said to the leader, "I know who you people are. And I want you to know although I do not support violence, I support your cause."

The leader's nose flared as he sucked air into his lungs. He turned to Father Dixon.

"Who do you think we are?"

Father Dixon stood erect, his hands together.

"I know of your movement and your cause is just. But if your cause is to survive, you must refrain from violence."

The leader raised his gun, pointing it at Father Dixon.

"We do not take orders from white men."

"I'm sorry. I did not mean that as an order. I only meant…"

The leader hit Father Dixon in the face with his rifle butt. The Father fell, hitting the ground hard. I scrambled to help him up. When he was on his feet, he shook his head. Blood ran from the corner of his mouth.

"Are you okay, Father?" I said.

He waved me away. "I'm okay."

He wasn't okay. He wobbled then almost fell over. I held him up, then turned to the leader.

"What the hell did you do that for?"

The leader raised his rifle as if to hit me then lowered it.

"One more word from you and I will kill you."

Father Dixon took a deep breath and put himself between me and the leader.

"This young man is a guest in our country, sir. Whatever your problems are with me don't apply to him."

The leader's eyes twitched when he said, "I will decide what applies to both of you."

Father Dixon managed a weak smile. "I know your people have been wronged and God sympathizes with your plight."

That angered the leader. He grabbed Father Dixon's collar and pulled him close.

"You know nothing of me or our cause," he said, spitting his words. "Your God is a white God who does not speak for my people." The leader stood erect, raising his head in a proud way to look down on Father Dixon. "Your white churches have turned against us as all white men do."

Father Dixon seemed to realize he'd said the wrong thing.

"You're right. You're right. Many churches have not supported your cause. But the church I belong to has always been the friend of the African people."

The leader considered what Father Dixon said. But I could tell he wasn't buying it.

"You are like all white men. You would say anything to save yourself. Even turn against your own kind."

I wanted nothing to do with this argument. I didn't know what it was about and didn't want to stick around for the outcome. Whatever the problem was between Father Dixon and these people, it looked like it wasn't going to end well. I started looking around for an escape.

The leader stepped back. He handed his gun to one of his men and took the man's machete. The leader turned to Father Dixon. He pointed the machete at the Father's face. When he spoke, the leader's voice was low, threatening.

"I do not care what church you belong to. I do not care what you think you know of my cause. The only thing I care about is you are a white man, and it is time all white men must leave Africa or die." The leader leaned forward, his machete at Father Dixon's throat. "Tell me, Father, when will you be leaving Africa?"

Father Dixon fell to his knees, his open hands to the sky.

"Please, understand. I was born here. This country is as much mine as it is yours."

This enraged the man. He stepped back, an evil look in his eyes. He leaned forward, speaking through clenched teeth.

"You think you belong in this country as much as we do? My people have been here since the beginning of time. All of you whites are invaders in my country. You don't belong here."

Father Dixon began to cry. He was shaking, pleading, "Please, I meant no disrespect. I am a simple man of God, and I love this country as much as you do. And I want justice for you and your kind so we can all live in…"

Father Dixon never finished the sentence. As he was talking, the leader swung his machete. It sliced through the Father's throat with such ease, Father Dixon's body remained upright for a moment. Father Dixon grabbed his throat where the blade had cut through half his neck. Blood shot through his fingers, spraying the man who had just dealt him a death blow. The Father dropped face first into the dirt, a pool of blood spreading around his body. The gang roared, raising their guns and machetes in the air.

I shouted at the leader, "Are you out of your mind?"

The leader wheeled around to me. I had heard about blood lust but had no experience with it. Whatever it was, this man had it. The look on his face was beyond that of a predator. It was a mask of contorted fury.

I was too stunned to move. The only time I ever saw anyone killed was in the movies. Believe me, it isn't the same as seeing it in real life. An electric surge rushed through my body. I started to tremble. I couldn't catch a breath. The leader raised the blood-stained machete over his head. He was about to drive it into my skull when the words jumped out of my mouth. I yelled, "Stop, I'm J.A. Quill's son."

To my amazement, the machete froze midair.

The leader did not move. Glared at me. Turned to his gang. I got a dozen eyes focused on me like they had just seen a ghost.

"What did you say?"

I held up my hands in defense. I spoke calmly, trying to add some threat to my words. But they came out pinched, unsteady.

"I told you. I'm J.A. Quill's son. Do you know who you're messing with?" I didn't know, but he certainly did. His gang traded worried glances. The leader slowly lowered the machete. The man was clearly afraid.

"What is your name?" he asked.

I was shaking but still tried to sound as angry as I could. "I am Jack Andrew Quill, son of one J.A. Quill. And it appears you know who he is." I hoped he didn't ask me where my father was. "And you better not mess with me."

The leader gave me the once over.

"You do look like J.A." He turned to his companions. "He does look like J.A., doesn't he?"

Nods, agreement, all around. I've only seen smiles like that at birthday parties.

Still keeping an eye on me, the leader handed the bloody machete to the man behind him. He reached out to shake my hand. My hand was trembling when I returned the invitation.

"I used to work for your father," the leader said. "He's an old friend of mine."

Without thinking, I told him, "Yeah, me too."

That got a laugh.

"So, Jack," the leader said, "where are you headed?"

"To Nairobi?" I said, uncertain of everything at that moment.

"We would give you a ride but unfortunately we have business elsewhere."

"That's... that's okay. I'll be okay. Okay?"

He nodded.

The leader looked at the Father's lifeless body.

"I'm sorry you had to see that. But this man represents the enemy of my people. And if you stay in this country long enough, you will understand why I had to do what I did."

I shrugged. "I don't plan to stay too long."

He turned to his gang. "All right everyone. Let's go."

The gang climbed into the truck. Driver got in and started the engine. The leader kept looking me over. He smelled of blood and gunpowder.

He smiled and said, "Do me a favor, Jack."

When I nodded, my head seemed to bounce like a rubber ball.

"Sure," I said.

"If you tell your father about this, let him know I spared you because of my friendship with him."

"Okay."

He jumped in the truck. They drove away, continuing to shout something I didn't understand.

I fell to my knees beside Father Dixon's body. A pool of blood spread around him. I felt sick to my stomach. I touched him, hoping he might still be alive. No reaction. No pulse. I didn't know what to do. I looked around to see if there was someone who might help. No one in sight. I couldn't control my breathing. I had to do something.

I carefully turned the Father's body over. His eyes were still open, as if pleading with me to save him. Tears streamed down my face. Even though I had only known Father Dixon for a short time, the idea of a living, breathing human being cut down like an animal struck me so hard I doubled over into an uncontrollable fit of crying. I stayed there until I became aware the sun was fading fast.

I couldn't leave Father Dixon's body where he fell, knowing there were animals in the area. I picked him up and carried him back to the station building. I was still in shock from witnessing his murder. I had to stop several times to rest. If there were lions roaming about, I would be easy prey.

When I finally made it to the train depot, I managed to pry open a door. Inside was no first-class hotel but it was safe enough until the next day when I hoped to the catch the train to Nairobi. The Father's body would be secure in the station until the train arrived.

I placed him near a wall with his arms folded over his chest. Then I remembered his Bible. I hurried back to the spot where the leader threw it away. I found it and returned to the station where I placed the book in one of the Father's hands. Father Dixon's eyes and mouth were open as if he was about to say something. I closed his eyes, took off my jacket, and covered his face.

I heard voices. I opened the door and peeked out. Two women were passing by not far away. They were laughing and carrying baskets on their heads. I couldn't risk asking them for help. I closed the door and settled down for a long wait.

When the sun dropped below the horizon, the animal sounds began. Lions roaring not far away. A distant elephant trumpet call. I tried to sleep, but the memory of the machete ripping through Father Dixon's throat was a repeating nightmare. I tossed and turned, trying to make sense of what had happened. Father Dixon was obviously a good man, a gentle man, a man of peace. Who would harm such a man? What kind of crazy world was this place? All I wanted was to find my father, make him pay for breaking my mother's heart and go home. How much more insanity would I have to suffer before I could leave this God-forsaken country? Little did I know.

14.

I WOKE NEXT MORNING to people talking. Father Dixon's body was already giving off an odor. I had to get him on the train as soon as possible. I checked my watch. It was nearly 7 a.m. The train ride from Mombasa to Nairobi takes about fifteen hours. If it left on time, it should arrive here at the station about 7:30 or 8.

I opened the door to the depot. There were three people standing outside. Two African women and a man. They saw me. I smiled. They smiled, surprised. I stepped out of the building.

"Good morning," I said.

They nodded, keeping a careful eye on me. I closed the door behind me.

"What time is the train due?" I asked.

The man spoke. "Very soon."

"It will stop here, won't it?"

"Yes sir," the man said. The women seemed uncomfortable.

"I got off the train yesterday and didn't get back on," I said.

They stared.

"Are you people here to catch the train?"

The man said, "Yes sir."

A train whistle blew. They hurried toward the tracks, giving me a wide berth. I couldn't blame them. I must have scared hell out of them coming out of an abandoned shack in the middle of nowhere.

When the train slowed to a stop, a conductor appeared. The three people handed him tickets and scrambled onto the train, glancing at me with suspicion. I found my first-class ticket in my pocket. When I handed it to the conductor, he looked at it and said, "Where the bloody hell did you come from?"

I explained I had a difference with some passengers who forced me to leave the train yesterday and I had to spend the night in the Athi River depot. The conductor glanced at the rundown building.

"You spent the night in there?"

"Yes sir," I said.

"That's bonkers." He shook his head and motioned me into the train.

"Before I board," I said, "is there a policeman on the train?"

"You mean a bobby?"

"If that's a policeman, yes."

"What do you need a bobby for?" he asked.

"It's best I explain to the authorities what happened to me."

The conductor raised eyebrows. Shook his head again, disappeared into the train. The engine made a hissing sound. The conductor returned with a man dressed in a suit wearing a funny hat.

"Who are you?" he asked.

"My name is Jack. Are you a policeman? I mean a bobby?"

His head moved back, revealing a double chin. "I beg your pardon."

I glanced at the conductor. "I asked the conductor if there was a policeman on board."

The man was obviously insulted.

He said, "I am Inspector Harris. State your business."

"I need to talk to you in private, sir," I said. "It's very important." I looked at the conductor. "And the train must stay here until I talk with the Inspector."

The two men traded confused glances. The Inspector shot a warning look at me.

"This had better be important."

I followed them into the train, dreading the story I had to tell. We found an empty sleeper. The Inspector closed the door. We sat opposite each other. He waited for me to speak. I cleared my throat. My nerves were on edge. I took a deep breath.

"I witnessed a murder yesterday, sir."

The Inspector didn't blink. He reached into a pocket and pulled out a notebook and pencil. The man probably had a lot of experience with murder. He looked at me and nodded. As I told my story, he took notes.

I recounted everything that had happened. How Harry, and Arthur and Sir-What's-His-Name had kicked me off the train the day before at the depot here in Athi River. How I met Father Dixon passing by, and about the gang who killed him and how they spared me. I didn't tell him why they spared me and he didn't ask. I explained how I carried the Father's body to the depot and spent the night.

"Father Dixon's in the depot," I told him. "Someone's got to do the right thing and recover his body."

"What did you say your name was?" he asked.

"Jack."

His pencil paused over the notebook.

"Jack what?"

The question I dreaded. I knew better than to lie to the authorities. I was facing enough trouble as it was.

"Jack Quill."

The Inspector didn't react to my last name. "I need to see some identification," he said.

I dug my passport out of my backpack. He thumbed through the pages, then handed it to me. He wrote something in his notebook. When he finished, he looked me over. He had the sort of face you'd expect from a policeman. No expression, no smile creases, only official looking deadpan eyes.

"So, Mr. Quill. What is your business in Africa?"

The second question I dreaded. I plunged in, hoping for the best.

"I'm here to find my father."

"Who is your father?"

I mumbled, "J.A. Quill."

The Inspector gave me a sideways glance. He wrote in his notebook. Closed it, put it and the pencil in his pocket.

I asked him, "Do you know my father?"

He stood.

"That will be all, Mr. Quill."

I asked him, "Am I under arrest?"

"No," the Inspector said.

I blinked and stuttered. "Really? You believe me?"

"Yes. The gang you described that killed this Father Dixon. They were apprehended yesterday not far from where you said the priest was killed. They murdered a farmer and his wife and a farmhand. Hacked them to death. Before they could get away, they were caught by the authorities. We've been after them for days."

"I thought they were going to kill me too," I said.

"You're American. Their disagreements are with the British."

I knew not to tell him the real reason they didn't kill me.

"I'm glad you caught them," I said. "What they did to Father Dixon was awful." I breathed a big sigh of relief. "By the way, why would anyone want to kill a priest?"

"It's complicated," he said. "Being a visitor in our country, it's best not to ask any more questions about that." The inspector relaxed, crossed his legs. Put his notebook away. "Now, as for you, where are you headed?"

"Nairobi."

"If I wanted to get in touch with you, where will you be?"

"The Norfolk hotel."

"Why the Norfolk?"

I wiped away the sweat on my face. "I worked for a man named Mr. Nagata at a zoo in Virginia. He told me when I got to Nairobi to look up a Mr. Cole at the Norfolk hotel."

The Inspector perked up. "Nagata, huh? I remember a Nagata fellow from the old days when I was a safari guide. We used to call him Blinky. A real good chap." His mood faded. "As for Mr. Cole..." The Inspector stood. "We need to get some men to retrieve Father Dixon's body. You'll excuse me."

"So, I'm free to go?"

The Inspector gave me a fatherly look. "You did the right thing, son. Just make sure when you get to Nairobi you watch your back."

The Inspector left the room. His last words stuck with me. Watch your back? As it turned out, I should have listened to him.

15.

THE SOUND OF SQUEALING brakes meant we had arrived at the Nairobi train station. The engineer pulled the whistle. All hell broke loose.

It was early morning when hundreds of passengers scrambled to bail out of the third-class cars through windows and doors. The Nairobi station was quickly swamped with mobs of travelers. Waves of people pushing, shoving, shouting. The first-class passengers waited for the crowds to clear. I didn't. I grabbed my pack and pushed through the outside door into the chaos. After a ruined dinner, a possible romance gone bad, kicked off the train, and being a witness to a murder, I couldn't wait to get on with my business.

I waded into the swirling mass of bodies. I hoped to find my way before sundown to the Norfolk hotel and Mr. Phillip Cole. I pushed forward through the crush with no luck. A flood of people swept over me like a human title wave. Something or someone elbowed me in the jaw. I took a nosedive onto the platform with a virtual stampede rolling over me. Tried to stand but got knocked down again. A forest of legs overran me. Someone tried to wrench my pack from my shoulder. I hung on as long as I could but lost the battle. I watched a hand whisk it away only to see another hand take it back. My pack became the object of a fight. When I thought all was lost, a more powerful arm swept the intruders aside. Someone reached down and plucked me out of the thicket of bodies. A moment later, I dangled at the end of the longest arm I'd ever seen attached to a man. An African man, nearly seven feet tall. Hair in braids, bright red tunic, intense eyes, and a wicked-looking spear. He was like a warrior. He handed me my pack.

"Thank you," I said.

He stared at me a moment then walked away. The crowd thinned.

I shouted. "Hey. Sir. Sir."

He turned, gave me a look.

"Do you know where the Norfolk hotel is?"

The man pointed.

"Thank you, sir. Thank you."

The warrior walked away.

"Oh, sir," I yelled. "One more thing. Do you know a man named Phillip Cole?"

He stopped, his back still to me. Then he continued on.

"I guess that's a no."

I slung my pack over my shoulder and started walking in the direction the man pointed. My first day in Nairobi and I had already made a friend.

16.

IT TOOK ME THE better part of an hour to find the hotel. I struggled past rows of cars, through a downtown development, past private homes. Finally reached an open field and my first view of the Norfolk hotel.

It was a broad building with a pitched roof entrance. I headed for the ornate front doors.

Inside, lavish furniture, sofas, lamps, expensive rugs decorated the reception room. Black and white photographs lined the walls depicting older days of safaris, hunters, animals, and a photo of the hotel in what appeared like earlier times. In the lobby, a few guests sat on couches reading magazines, drinking cups of coffee or maybe tea. I'd never checked into a hotel before. I hadn't even been in one. So, this is the way rich people live, I thought.

A young woman stood behind the front desk. She was all smiles as I approached.

"Good afternoon, sir. Are you checking in?"

A British accent. The girl wore a pin that said Shirley.

"Yeah. I need a room."

"Do you have a reservation?"

"No, I don't," I told her. "Do I need one?"

She smiled. "What's your name?"

"Jack. Jack Sims."

"Let's see what's available, Mr.Sims."

She opened a large book. Ran her finger over lists. While she checked her records, I noticed more pictures behind her. I couldn't get over all the old pictures in the place. Photos of ancient looking trains. More old pictures of a town which I assumed was Nairobi. And there were a couple of huge rifles hanging on hooks. A loud crash came from a room to my right. I peered in. An explosion of laughter.

"What's going on in there?" I asked Shirley.

"Oh, that's a party in the bar. The East African Professional Hunters Association." She seemed annoyed. "They have a blowout every time one of them bags an elephant." She smirked. "They drink a lot."

Another outburst of shouting, laughter.

I asked, "They celebrate the killing of elephants?"

"Yes. They also celebrate celebrating." She closed her record book. "We do have one room left," she said.

"Good," I said. "I guess I'll take it."

She leaned forward, whispering. "But it's expensive."

I must have looked like someone who couldn't afford expensive. I confirmed that by asking, "How much?"

In a normal voice, she asked, "You're American, aren't you?"

"Yeah."

"I'll give it to you in dollars."

I couldn't get enough of her smiles. She picked up a pencil. Scribbled on a notepad. The amount surprised me.

"Am I buying the room?" I asked.

She giggled.

"No. It's just for one night."

I still had about two hundred dollars in my pack. I hadn't really thought of how long I would need to stay in Africa. How much time does it take to avenge a broken heart?

"Okay. So, you do take American money?"

"Of course."

"I guess I can afford a couple of nights."

I dug into my pack, feeling for my wallet. Nothing. I opened the flap, peered in. My toilet kit, a book, some maps of Africa, my clothes. But not the wallet. Panic. I turned the kit upside down, pouring the contents onto the front desk. Out dumped all my belongings. Pants, socks, a pair of sneakers, three shirts and a couple of pairs of underwear.

"What the hell?" I said.

Shirley backed away as if I'd just dumped a dozen snakes on her desk. My heart pounded. I shook my head.

"My wallet. All my money. It's gone."

"Sir, I'm so sorry. Do you remember where...?"

I interrupted her. "The train station. They took my money at the train station."

"Who took your money?"

I tried to focus.

"A tall guy. He wore a bright red robe. He had a spear."

Shirley shook her head. "You just described a Maasai warrior. They don't steal."

"Then it must have been one of those passengers who pushed me down."

"I'm so sorry, sir," she said.

I sat on the floor, leaned against the front desk. Shirley came around to help.

"Do you have any place you can go? Any friends? Any relatives?"

I tried to clear my head. Nothing came to mind. Then I was about to mention Mr. Nagata's friend, Mr. Cole, when I heard a loud smack. Shouting, scuffling, more hits. Laughter growing louder. A tumble of bodies rolled into the lobby from the bar. A half-dozen men dressed in bush hats, khakis, scuffed-up boots teetering like the staggering drunks they were. Arm in arm, swinging at each other, connecting, falling into a mass of bodies. Those who could stand wobbled to their feet waving beer bottles. The few that were so drunk they couldn't stand fell back on their knees, bottles to their mouths. They all started to sing.

"To Anacreon in heaven, where he sat in full glee, a few sons of harmony sent a petition that he, their inspirer and patron would be..."

It took me a minute to realize the melody of this drinking song was very much like the melody of America's "The Star-Spangled Banner." When they finished, I spoke to the man who was leading the song. He was an older gentleman wearing a beret. Had a big rifle slung over his shoulder. A beer mug in his hand. He was trying to help one of his drunken companions to his feet.

"Pardon me, sir," I said.

The old guy took another sip from his mug, sloshing beer on his jacket.

I raised my voice. "Hello, sir."

His fallen friend was passed out. The old man had trouble picking up dead weight.

"Sir. Hello there," I said, almost shouting.

He turned to me, still tugging on his buddy's arm.

"Who the hell are you?" His words slurred. He stared at me through bloodshot eyes.

I held out my hand. "I'm Jack Sims, sir. And you are...?"

"I say, chap, could you give me some help here?"

I grabbed the boozer he was trying to help and lifted him to his feet. His plastered friends struggled to keep him upright. The old man dropped his friend's arm and shook my hand.

"Thank you, young man. Good to make your acquaintance. I am Reginald Downey. Reggie to me friends."

He shook my hand.

"By the way, sir," I said. "That song you were singing. It's very much like the melody to the American national anthem."

Reggie put his hands on his hips and sneered at me.

"For your information, young fellow, the United States of America stole that tune from us."

"Who's us?" I asked.

He looked at his drinking buddies. They laughed. He said to me, "You're a Yank, aren't you?"

"I'm an American."

"Well, we didn't mean to offend you by stealing your song, which, as I said, belonged to Great Britain first." He downed the last of his drink. "But I'll tell you what. Just to apologize for our musical indiscretions, we'll show you the respect you deserve."

Reggie swung around to face his ginned-up songbirds.

"Okay, boys. Let's show the Yank some good old British hospitality. The Star-Spangled banana, please."

I protested, "The Star-Spangled Banner."

Reggie answered with a slur. "That's what I said, old chap."

Reggie led his boozed-out chorus in singing the United States national anthem. His boys joined in one by one. I was surprised they knew the lyrics. I put my hand over my heart and sang along. As soused as they were, they almost got it right except the end. When we finished singing home of the brave, the entire bleary-eyed entourage applauded.

Reggie approached me, took me by the shoulders and asked, "So, Yank, how did we do?"

I nodded approval. "Pretty good except it's not 'home of the braves.' It's 'home of the brave.'"

"Well, I deeply regret our transgression," he said, his alcoholic breath almost knocking me over. "You Yanks saved our sorry asses during the Great War. The least we can do is sing your goddamned song right."

Before I could tell him it wasn't necessary, he had his group of tin ears sing the entire national anthem again, only this time they shouted the last six words. "And the home of the brave."

The drunken misfits applauded.

"Thank you, sir." I said, "By the way, you're a hunter, aren't you?"

Reggie laughed. "What gave me away? The hat or the gun?"

"The gun," I said. "The hat makes you look silly."

That gave his buddies a chuckle.

I continued. "Would you or your friends happen to know a man by the name of Phillip Cole?"

Reginald and his buddies went cold sober. They let a shit-faced gentleman they were supporting fall to his knees. The looks they gave me meant I'd stepped into private territory.

"What's your business with Mr. Cole?" Reginald asked, squinting at me.

"Do you know him?"

"I didn't say I did, and I didn't say I didn't."

"Is that a maybe or a maybe not?" I asked.

"Maybe."

There was a definite air of distrust in the room.

"Well, you see," I continued, "there's this man back home in Virginia where I'm from in America. And this man, Mr. Nagata, told me when I got to Nairobi, I should look up Mr. Phillip Cole at the Norfolk hotel. Mr. Nagata's an old friend of his."

"Who the hell is Mr. Na-gaah-ta?" Reginald asked in a not so friendly way. I remember wishing Reginald would remove his grip on the rifle. I regretted calling his hat silly.

"It's Nagata not Na-gaah-ta," I said. I continued. "As I said, he's an old friend of Mr. Cole's."

"Don't remember anyone by that name," Reginald said.

He turned to his companions. They swayed in their drunkenness like trees in the wind. Some almost fell.

Reginald asked them, "Anybody here ever heard of a Mr. Na-gaah-ta?"

"Nagata," I said, with emphasis, "Nagata."

He lowered his head, peered at me through barely opened eyes. Reginald's sunny disposition turned mean.

"Look here, friend, you're starting to get on me nerves. We don't know this Na-gaah-ta guy so if you don't mind, you need to piss off before I really get angry."

His right hand dropped to the trigger of his rifle. I imagined crosshairs on my face. Then I was reminded of the nickname Mr. Nagata told me to use.

"You might recall Mr. Nagata by his nickname," I said.

"And what the bloody hell is his goddamned nickname?" Reginald said.

"Blinky. That's what Mr. Cole called Mr. Nagata. Blinky."

Reggie's friends repeated the name to each other as if they were recalling a long-lost brother. Reginald gave me a big grin, and the gang went all smiles. He turned to his one of his barely conscious shit-faced companions on his knees.

"Hey, Phil old buddy. You hear that? This mate knows Blinky."

The shit-faced guy had his arm wrapped around the knee of a buddy to keep from falling over.

"Is that Mr. Phillip Cole?" I asked.

Reginald went over and slapped the man's face.

"Phil? You hear me? There's someone here talking about Blinky."

I assumed the one he called Phil was Mr. Cole. Mr. Cole opened bloodshot eyes. He settled on Reginald.

"Huh?" Mr. Cole was drooling.

Reggie got in Mr. Cole's face, talking as if to a five-year-old. "Phillip?" He gave him another gentle slap in the face. "Focus, man. This boy knows Blinky. Remember Blinky?"

All Mr. Cole could manage through the fog of drunkenness is one word. "Huh?" He took a breath and collapsed on the floor. Reginald motioned to a couple of the more sober men in the group.

"Get Phil to his office."

Two big hunters lifted Mr. Cole as far as they could. They ended up dragging him away.

Reginald turned his attention to me.

"Sonny, next time you see Blinky tell my old friend he owes Reginald Downey ten bloody quid."

I was already following the guys dragging Mr. Cole down the hall.

17.

THE TWO MUSCLE MEN dragged Mr. Cole through a narrow hallway to an office. I followed them into a large room filled with stuffed animals of all types. Trophies of lions, gazelle, cheetah, zebra. Two enormous elephant tusks framed the doorway. The two men dumped Mr. Cole onto a large leather chair behind a mahogany desk. On the front of the desk was the carved figure of a lion.

"Have a seat, kid," one of the big guys said. "He'll be out for a while."

They left me with Mr. Cole, his arms draped over his chair, his head on his chest. He started to snore. I took a seat in a wooden chair on the other side of the desk. After a few minutes, I fell asleep. More than an hour later, I woke up with Mr. Cole hovering over me wild-eyed and looking mean.

"Who the hell are you?"

I stood, held out a hand. He ignored it. So far, I'd had too much trouble being known as J.A. Quill's son. I avoided giving him my real name for now.

"Jack Sims," I told him.

"What the hell are you doing in my office?" Mr. Cole asked.

I backed off to escape the overpowering smell of alcohol. His breath could melt butter.

He went behind his desk, opened a drawer. Took out a bottle. He took a drink and sat down.

"Well, before I get to why I'm here…" I said.

Mr. Cole threw up a hand.

"Hold it. You're not a constable, are you?"

"What's a constable?"

"You're American."

I nodded.

"It's what you Americans call a cop."

"I thought a cop here was a bobby."

"Same thing," Mr. Cole said.

"Well, I'm not a constable or a cop."

"You a bill collector? Cause right now I'm sort of beggared."

"What does that mean?"

He frowned. "It means I'm broke." He hit the bottle again, eyeing me suspiciously. "You're not here to collect for my ex-wife, are you?"

I said, "Sir, I'm not a cop, I'm not a bill collector, and I don't know your ex-wife."

The trophies were spooking me. I circled the room.

Mr. Cole said, "Sit down. You're making me nervous."

I sat.

Mr. Cole said, "So if you're not a cop or a bill collector and you're not here 'cause I'm behind on my alimony, then what do you want from me?"

"I came to Nairobi on a personal matter, but when I got to Mombasa…" I stopped short of telling him about being kidnapped by Walter and kicked off the train by Harry and company. I especially didn't want to bring up the murder of Father Dixon.

"As I was about to say," I continued, "some locals mugged me at the train station this morning and stole all my money. I don't know where to turn."

"Look, chap. I don't know who you are, but I don't loan money to strangers."

"I'm not looking for a loan. I need a job so I can stay here until I find my father."

"Who's your father?"

"Never mind that. Are you going to help me?"

"I ain't no bank."

"I'm not asking for a loan."

He took another drink. Leaned across the desk, eyes riveted on me. "Then what the hell do you want from me cause whatever it is I can't help you."

"That's not what Mr. Nagata said."

"Who the hell is Mr. Nagata?"

"You don't remember in the lobby when I told Mr. Downey about Mr. Nagata?"

"I don't remember shit past an hour ago," he said. "I knew a girl named Charlotta but no guy named Nagata." That gave him a laugh.

"Mr. Nagata told me when I got here to look you up."

"Name doesn't ring a bell," Mr. Cole said.

"Do you remember a guy named Blinky?"

The mention of Blinky stopped him cold.

"What did you say?"

"Blinky. I know him as Mr. Nagata. He said he used to work for you. He told me you called him Blinky."

He paused, took a moment to think. Then a big smile and a bigger laugh. "Yeah, I knew a guy from the old days named Blinky." Mr. Cole's face brightened. His voice went up a pitch. "Old Blinky. Haven't heard that name in years." Mr. Cole slapped his knee and laughed. "Well, bloody hell. Of course, I remember him. How is the hell is old Blinky?"

"He's fine," I said.

"What the hell is that bloke doing these days?"

"He manages a zoo in the United States."

"Well, kiss my ass. Of course, he does." Mr. Cole turned to me with a big wide smile and said, "You know what Blinky used to do for me?"

"No sir."

"He was my gunbearer. And a pretty good one." He nodded at the wall trophies. "He bagged some of those. See those elephant tusks?"

I glanced at them.

"Those babies are record-class. Each about 130 pounds. Big bull elephant. Blinky took him with a .577 Westley Richards. Right between the eyes." He stared at the tusks, obviously enjoying the memory of the hunt. "You know why we called him Blinky?"

I shrugged.

"Every time he drew down on an animal he would hesitate. Always took too long. Hesitate, blink. Hesitate, blink. He missed a lot of shots. But I give him this. When he did shoot, he never missed."

I glanced at the large tusks again. "And Mr. Nagata shot the elephant those belonged to?"

Mr. Cole nodded. "Yeah. He was real good at killing elephants. That was a male, of course. There are rules against killing cows." He glanced at me. "Females, that is." Mr. Cole got serious. His eyes darted back and forth as if recalling a troubled memory. He drained the bottle he was holding, then threw it into a nearby trash can. He cleared his throat and took a deep breath.

"I remember this one incident when Blinky was forced to kill a cow. Something no professional hunter would ever do unless it was absolutely necessary. It happened about ten years ago near a place called Treetops Lodge. About sixty miles from here. We were stalking a bull elephant near the Lodge when we heard a scream."

Mr. Cole rummaged through his desk looking for something.

"Turned out two tourists, a man and his wife, wandered too far from the Lodge where they encountered a female elephant and her calf. The mother felt threatened and charged them. Blinky arrived just in time to save the couple from being killed. He shouldered his .577 Westley Richards on that poor creature and dropped it within inches of the frightened couple. It was the only time when Blinky didn't blink. He was the hero of the day. The couple couldn't stop thanking him for saving their lives. But when Blinky saw that calf..."

Cole stopped, studied me.

"You know what an elephant calf is?"

I shrugged.

"It's a baby. A thousand-pound baby elephant."

Mr. Cole opened a drawer. Found another bottle. It was almost empty. He finished it. When he continued the story, his voice was low, soft.

"Anyway, when Blinky saw this baby elephant crying over its dead mother..." Cole seemed embarrassed. "Yeah, elephants cry. At least it seems like they do."

He got solemn like he saw something in his mind's eye he didn't want to revisit. After an awkward pause, he took up where his memory left off.

"Well, the baby elephant climbed up on the back of its dead mother and started this chirping sound. God, it broke our hearts." His eyes moved around the room, scanning his trophies. "Blinky went crazy on us. He joined the baby by its mother. Tried to comfort it. Stayed with it for hours. It was getting dark, but he wouldn't leave the mother or that baby. So, we just pitched camp nearby. All night we heard the baby crying for its mother. All night Blinky stayed with it. Even ran into camp like some psycho taking food and water to it. We finally retired to our tents. I couldn't sleep. I tried to muffle the sounds of that pitiful creature by burying my head in a pillow. Whimpering all night. Come morning, Blinky was asleep on the mother's leg. The baby is still on top of its mother. Weeping."

Mr. Cole shook his head. Kept shaking it as if in a trance. He threw the empty bottle into the trash.

"What happened to the baby?" I asked.

He smiled. "That was the end of Blinky's hunting days. He left for America soon after that. Never heard from him again."

Mr. Cole didn't speak for a while.

"How many elephants have you shot?" I asked.

"Why are you asking?"

I glanced at the two large elephant tusks framing the door.

"When I was in Mombasa there was a mountain of ivory being loaded onto railroad cars. A man was auctioning them off for lots of money." I looked Mr. Cole square in the eyes. "Have you made a lot of money killing elephants? Selling their ivory?"

Mr. Cole glanced past me at the tusks then swung back to me with a murderous look in his eyes.

"You got a smart mouth, kid. You need to keep it shut about poaching. Talk like that can get you killed."

"I didn't mention poaching," I said.

"I think this conversation is over," he said.

"What happens to the ivory of elephants you kill?"

"It belongs to our clients."

"For trophies?"

Mr. Cole came around his desk. He zeroed in on me.

"Listen, buddy." He rolled his shoulders like he was shaking off a load of guilt. "Like I said, I ain't no poacher. I'm Phillip Pennington Cole the Third, President of the East African Professional Hunter's Association. Every kill we make is legal. And I have the reputation throughout Africa as a man of honor. I'm not a bloody poacher. Understand?"

I nodded. He went back to his desk. Ransacked his drawers for more liquor. Found another empty bottle. Threw it crashing against the wall. It took him awhile to calm down.

"You know what they call me?" Mr. Cole asked.

"No sir."

"The Great White Hunter. I was just awarded Hunter of the Year for 1952. Got it for dropping a bull elephant that charged me. He fell within ten feet of my stupid client. Shot right through the brain with my .350 Rigby Nitro Express. The tusks weighed 120 pounds each. Never missed a shot in my life."

"And they give awards for that?"

"Of course." He gave me a nasty look. "Is that a problem?"

I shrugged, careful not to tread on the hunter's code, whatever that was.

Finally, he said, "So, Blinky told you to look me up when you got here, huh?"

"Yes sir. He said you might even have a job for me."

"Well, you wasted a trip, son."

As much as I hated to do it, it was time to use my father's name to my advantage. I figured Dad must pull some weight in this country considering the reactions I'd gotten to his name. I just hoped he didn't owe Mr. Cole any money.

"Well, if you can't give me a job maybe you can help me find my father," I said.

Mr. Cole found another small bottle of whiskey about half full. "Whadda you know. Where'd that come from?" He took a drink. Made a face. He asked me, "Your father? Is he lost?"

"Is he what?"

"You said you want me to help you find your father." He punched the air with the bottle. "Is he lost?"

"He is to me."

"Is he in Kenya?"

"The last letter we received from him was from Nairobi. It was written on Norfolk hotel stationery."

"Who's we?"

"Me and my mother."

"You came all the way from America to find dear ol' dad? How sweet."

He took another drink.

"I'm not looking forward to it."

"Sounds like you and your dad aren't on good terms."

"He left me and my mom when I was just a kid. Said he was going to seek his fortune. That he'd come home when he got rich. He never did. He left us without a penny. My mom eventually died of a broken heart."

Mr. Cole looked at his watch. He stood. "Look, kid. It's a very sad story but I have a big safari leaving tomorrow and I've got to go meet the clients."

"Okay, but if you can't help me find my father, so how about that job? Like I told you, someone stole all my money."

Mr. Cole was getting testy. "I'm not hiring. Okay?"

He moved toward the door.

"I can help with your safari. I worked in a zoo and I know a lot about animals."

Mr. Cole stopped short of the door.

"Africa ain't no zoo. And these animals ain't in cages."

All I had left was begging.

"Please, Mr. Cole. I'm begging you. If I have to go home, I'll never find my father."

His head fell to his chest.

"Jesus, kid. You're a pain in the ass." He faced me. "What did you say your name was?"

"Jack Sims."

"I don't know anyone by the name of Sims."

I knew eventually if I expected him to help me I had to tell him who I really was. That was my ace in the hole. But after what had happened because of my real name, I knew I was taking a chance. I just hoped Mr. Nagata was right about Mr. Cole helping me.

"Sims is my mother's maiden name. The reason I've been using it is since I got here is because people get all weird when I mentioned my real name. I don't even want to go into what I've been through when I mentioned that."

Cole frowned. "So, what the hell is so important about your real name?"

I took a deep breath.

"My real name is Quill. Jack Quill."

Cole's eyes narrowed to a squint. "Did you say Quill?"

"Yeah."

His voice lost its edge. His eyes narrowed.

"What's your father's name?"

"J.A.," I said. "J.A. Quill."

Mr. Cole's face tightened. I thought, oh God, big mistake.

He cocked his head. "What was that name again?"

My throat knotted. "J.A. Quill."

Mr. Cole's eyes scanned the room like he was being watched. He twitched nervously.

"Where did you say you were from?"

"United States."

"Where in the United States?"

"Virginia."

He came around the desk. Studied my face like he was scanning a map.

Mr. Cole took a long drink from the bottle without taking his eyes off me. He squinted, nodded. Threw the bottle in the trash.

"Excuse me a minute, kid."

He turned and went into another room. Shut the door but accidentally left it slightly ajar. I could see he was on a phone. I couldn't hear what he was saying but he sounded nervous. He turned toward the door and saw me watching him. He hung up the phone and came back in the room. He gave me a forced smile.

"So, you need a job, huh?"

"Yes."

"Can you fix a car engine?"

"No."

"Have you ever shot a gun?"

"No."

"Do you know how to skin a kudu?"

"No, sir."

"You're hired."

Cole started toward the door then stopped.

"I've got a safari going out tomorrow morning. You're on it. 6 a.m. Outside the hotel. Don't be late."

"But I don't have any money. Where am I gonna stay?"

Mr. Cole dug into his pocket. Handed me a wad of bills.

"Go get something to eat. Then see the girl at the front desk. She'll set you up with a room." He starts out the door. "And get some bush clothes. You look like a damned tourist."

18.

THERE I WAS, STANDING in Mr. Cole's office with dozens of eyes staring at me. I'd had a lot of live animals at the zoo looking at me, but never this many dead ones. With Cole out of the office, I had an idea.

Mr. Nagata told me Mr. Cole would know where my father was. I had a suspicion Mr. Cole was on the phone with Dad. I should have confronted him about him knowing my father and where Dad was. But I didn't push my luck. There was always tomorrow.

There might be things in Cole's office that could help me find Dad. I went to his desk and started going through the drawers. There were several more bottles of whiskey, most of them almost empty. I'd never tasted whiskey before. I uncorked one of the bottles that had some left. I took a whiff. Almost knocked me over. I wanted to see if the taste was as potent as the smell.

I read the label on the bottle. I couldn't pronounce the name. It was made in Scotland. I took a drink. I remember getting into a fight at school when I was a kid. This bully punched me in the nose. That was the same feeling I got drinking whiskey. I coughed, almost gagged. It reminded me of western movies when a cowboy would go into a saloon, step up to the bar and ask for a whiskey. They would throw back a small glass of it as if they were drinking milk. So much for the honesty of Hollywood.

I put the bottle back and searched the other drawers. I came up with several files stuffed with business records. Invoices, lists of supplies, names of clients, and one file filled with photographs and newspaper clippings. I sorted through the photos and clippings. The clippings had several photos of a younger Mr. Cole. One showed him standing over a dead elephant with enormous tusks, a big rifle in his arms. There were more pictures of him with dead lions. I was about to put the newspaper clippings away when I uncovered a photo of Mr. Cole with a group of men all dressed in safari gear. They were smiling, arms around each other, standing over an enormous pile of elephant tusks. My eye caught a hunter standing to the side. It was my father, J.A. Quill. Mr. Cole had his arm around Dad, looking at him with a self-satisfied expression. But Dad was looking off to the side with a concerned look on his face.

Voices and footsteps in the hall broke my concentration. The sounds were headed my way. I quickly shoved the files in the drawers and looked around for a place to hide. The only place was the room where Mr. Cole had gone to make a phone call. I barely made it into the room when I heard someone enter the main office. I heard two men talking.

"So, what's their problem?" It was Mr. Cole.

I heard drawers being opened. The sound of glass on glass. Mr. Cole was probably having another drink.

Then, the other voice, higher than Mr. Cole's.

"They're complaining about the pay."

More glass clinking.

I heard footsteps. Sounds of someone pacing.

"Dammit, Ennis, I hired you to take care of these problems. Do whatever you have to but get me a crew. I can't afford to lose this safari."

"By the way, Mr. Cole," the man named Ennis said, "why is Mrs. Lewis going on this trip?"

"Why do you ask?" Mr. Cole said.

"You know who she works for. Do we need her nosing around?"

Mr. Cole sounded annoyed. "She's bringing her daughter along. They're on vacation. And it's none of your goddamned business."

"Sorry, boss."

"Besides, it's better we have her along where I can keep an eye on her. Just keep her occupied until I finish my business with Mason."

"Okay, boss."

"Now, let's go get the Rovers in place for tomorrow. And get me a crew."

"You got it."

Mr. Cole said, "You go ahead. I gotta make a phone call."

A door opened, closed.

Footsteps headed my way. I panicked. Looked around the room. There was a stuffed lion in the corner. It was posed on its haunches. The damned thing was bigger than a couch. I jumped behind it, laid flat just as Mr. Cole entered the room. I heard him pick up the phone and dial.

"Hey," Mr. Cole said. "Yeah, I know what you want me to do but I don't like it. Cause if something bad happens to him, I'm not taking the blame. By the way, this is the last favor I do for you. And when I meet up with your guy, he'd better have my money or I will…"

I heard clicking.

"Hello?"

More clicking then the sound of a phone being slammed on its cradle.

"Son-of-a-bitch."

Mr. Cole left.

I got up, patted the stuffed lion on its head.

"What did we get ourselves into?"

19.

SHIRLEY GOT ME A room. It was in the dark hotel basement, next to steam pipes knocking and clanging all night. No windows and a cot. She had someone bring a change of clothes. Khaki pants, a bush jacket, flannel shirt, terai hat. I don't know where she got them, but they weren't new. I only hoped an elephant killer hadn't worn them. I wanted to avoid guilt by association.

I got room service brought to me by a very nice kitchen worker. A sandwich with meat I'd never seen before. A bowl of local food called corn posho vaguely resembling oatmeal. And a Coca Cola. I could have used a hamburger and french fries. But at least I had my coke. It felt good to have something from home.

As things were turning out, my plan of revenge against my father wasn't going well. My first two days in Nairobi were a complete disaster. Loss of my money. Kidnapped by Walter and David. Embarrassment on the train. The murder of Father Dixon that would haunt me for the rest of my life. And now Mr. Cole who only helped me when I mentioned my father's name.

What power did my father have over people that caused them to fear him? I dismissed the thought he might be a criminal. That I couldn't imagine. Maybe he had discovered King Solomon's mines with its diamonds and gold. A millionaire with the sort of control rich people can have over the lives of normal people.

It was in that hotel basement of clanging pipes and bad food and no windows I realized that whatever he had become, I was torn between protecting the memory of a father I once loved and the one I had come to despise for what he did to my mother. No matter how things turned out, I would always have that one moment we shared that had become the only bond that linked me to the father I once knew and loved. That memory was like a light in a dark tunnel. It had seen me through a lot of bad times.

I went upstairs to the front desk. Shirley was on duty, bright and cheerful as ever.

I asked her, "Shirley, you have a paper and pen?"

She smiled. "Of course, Mr. Sims."

She opened a drawer, pulled out a sheet of Norfolk Hotel letterhead and gave me a fountain pen. It was the same type of letterhead my father used in his last letter to my mother. I carefully wrote something on the paper and handed it to Shirley. When she read it, her brow wrinkled.

"Would you read it to me?" I asked.

She looked at the scribbling again. "Really?"

I nodded.

She shrugged. "Okay."

She cleared her throat. Gave me a strange look. Shook her head and read it to me. "Doctor Livingstone, I presume?"

I said, "Could you sort of lower your voice and give me your best British accent?"

She cocked her head. "Alright."

She licked her lips. They were beautiful lips. Sort of sexy. Then she did what I asked. She managed as deep a delivery as she could.

"Doctor Livingston, I presume?"

She gave me a toothy smile.

"Great," I said, "but could you go a little lower?"

She frowned. "You want lower?"

"Yeah," I said.

She rolled her shoulders like she was about to go athletic. Pursed her lips. God, they were sexy. What came out was as close as a woman could get to what I felt captured the essence of Henry Morton Stanley's famous greeting to Doctor Livingston.

Her voice was low and gravelly. "Doctor Livingston, I presume?"

She looked at me for approval.

"Perfect," I said. "Thank you."

She smiled. "You're welcome."

20.

I WENT TO MY basement room and ate a leftover sandwich for dinner. After I finished, I thought I'd take a walk. Get to know the place.

The stairs led up to the same hallway where Mr. Cole's office was. Down the hallway was the hotel lobby. As I got close to the lobby, I heard the faint sound of a woman crying.

I entered the lobby and saw her. Her back was to me. She sat on one of the plush sofas crying. There was no one else in the room.

I moved to where I could see her face. She must have heard the squeak of my boots. She turned and looked at me. Tears stained her cheeks. She quickly wiped away her tears with a handkerchief. For a moment, she didn't recognize me. Then she smiled.

"You're the boy from the train," she said.

I nodded.

She said in a perfect British accent, "I see you have a fresh change of clothes."

"Yeah. I got tired of walking around with a shirt decorated with soup."

She laughed. I moved to the other side of the couch and sat down.

"Are you okay?" I asked.

"I suppose so."

"Why are you crying?"

"I sometimes cry when I'm happy."

"Do you laugh when you're sad?"

"Very funny," she said.

"So, what are you happy about?"

She perked up. "I'm going on a vacation with my mother." She wiped away the last of her tears. "I'm just so happy she finally trusts me to go with her on a safari."

She had dimples on a face so pure it muddled my thoughts. I couldn't think of anything important to say so, of course, I said something stupid.

"You don't get out much, do you?"

She gave me a half smile, a cock of the head.

"Do you always ask girls who cry in hotels silly questions?"

I must have blushed. "I don't see many girls in hotels."

She giggled. "You really made a mess on the train."

"I'll never live that down."

"I thought it was charming."

"So, you like boys who make fools of themselves?"

"Who said I like you?"

"Where's a bowl of soup when I need it?"

"You're American, aren't you?"

"Yeah," I said.

"I've never known an American," she said. "Especially an American boy."

"Well, as you've already noticed, we have unique ways of introducing ourselves to girls by turning over tables and spilling soup on ourselves."

Again, the laugh. Music to my ears.

"Where are you from in America?" she asked.

"Virginia."

"What kind of place is Virginia?"

"Like here only without the accent."

She giggled. "You're funny."

"I find humor has a way of breaking the ice between people."

She smirked. "Oh, you think you've broken the ice between us, do you?"

She gave me a challenging smile.

I folded my arms and fake shivered. "I take it back. It's getting cold in here."

She broke out laughing. A door opened behind me. Footsteps. The girl stopped laughing, her eyes looking past me. I turned to see the older woman who was with the girl on the train. She focused on me.

"Who are you?" she said.

Another British accent only this one had a bite to it.

The girl jumped up. I did the same.

The older woman moved between me and the girl.

She said to the girl, "I told you not to talk to strangers." She was one scary woman. A voice as low as a man's. But a beauty. She turned on me.

"I asked you. Who the hell are you?"

"Nobody in particular."

She came right at me.

"You're the idiot from the train."

"That's me," I said.

"I don't like you."

"But you don't know me."

"It's the company you were with I don't like."

"Oh, those guys. I'd just met them."

She moved closer. Close enough for me to smell her perfume. It was something a woman would wear, but only a very intimidating woman.

"You're a liar. I saw you buddying up to them. I know what you were talking about."

"How could you? You were too far away."

"Because I know the type of men they are. And that means you're just like them."

"Like I said, I'd just met them."

She had angry eyes. "Yeah, right. Just enough time to make your deal and move on to the next kill."

"The next what?" I said.

She pushed me. I reeled back on my heels, wondering what the hell was wrong with this woman. In fact, that's what I asked her.

"What the hell is wrong with you?"

She punched my chest with a finger. No one wants that when a woman has long nails.

"You stay the hell away from my daughter."

I learned in high school girls like a man with a strong personality. A man who would stand up for himself. Girls admire that. I gathered whatever strength I figured would impress the girl and maybe even her overbearing mother. Big mistake.

"Now look here," I said to her mother in a stern voice that sounded phony, "she is a grown woman and I'm a grown man and I don't think you have any business interfering with..."

The mother grabbed me by my lapels, choking off my words. She dragged me toward a door. Considering I towered over her, she had no trouble manhandling me. The girl followed, begging her to leave me alone. The mother let go of me momentarily, turned to the girl, grabbed her, and forced her onto the couch. Then she returned to me. Got hold of my arm, put a palm to my back and shoved me outside onto a stone patio. She wheeled me around, tightening her grip on my collar. This was one strong woman.

"You listen to me you little poaching bastard. If I ever see you close to my daughter again, I will drive one of your illicit tusks up your criminal ass. You hear me?"

"Ma'am, I think you've mistaken me for..."

She twisted my collar, choking me. "Shut up. I will make it my life's purpose to put all of you murderers in jail."

Gagging, I said, "I don't know what you're talking about."

She socked me in the jaw so hard it knocked the wind out of me. That's when my legs gave out. I fell to the stone floor of the patio. Hit my head on something solid. The rest I don't remember.

21.

I WOKE UP TO light and the sensation of flying. Tossed about like an out-of-control airplane. My eyes opened. Earth, inches from my face, rushing by. Voices, shouting, engines coughing, sputtering, turning over. I craned my neck, trying to see the aircraft I had boarded and why it was flying so close to the ground. I feared this plane was about to crash.

I looked up. A long black arm reaching from the sky extended from a bright red tunic clutching my jacket. That's when I realized it wasn't an airplane. I was being carried by someone.

The hand released me. I crashed to the ground. My mouth tasted of stale blood and dirt. I raised my head. Hovering over me, the giant man in the red tunic. The same warrior from the train station. Off to the right, a line of cars.

Mr. Cole's voice. "What happened to you, kid?"

I pushed to my feet. Unbearable pain. I staggered, got my balance. Cleared my head and tried to focus. The warrior and Mr. Cole stared at me. Past them, a row of six Land Rovers, motors running. I counted several people. Some were obviously there to work. Others dressed in safari outfits looked like tourists.

"Where am I?"

"Who'd you tangle with, boy?" Cole asked. "Looks like you got the shit end."

I straightened, military style. "Sorry, sir. I hope I'm not late."

"Well, you are." He pointed to the warrior. "This is Baako, my gunbearer."

Another man, a bearded, sullen looking man, approached. "This is Ennis, my safari manager. Do what he says."

Ennis, the man I heard in the room talking to Mr. Cole. He looked like a person who had probably broken some laws. Mr. Cole walked toward the cars. He got a few feet away and turned. I hadn't moved. Neither had the man he called Baako.

Mr. Cole put his hands on his hips. "Well? What are you waiting for?"

I looked at Ennis. "For him to tell me what to do."

Mr. Cole nodded at Ennis. Ennis motioned for me to follow. We headed toward the line of six safari cars. He stopped at the lead car. He pointed to the front seat.

"What?" I said.

He was chewing something. Mr. Cole came up behind me.

"What's the problem?"

"I don't know what he wants me to do."

Cole sighed. "You're gonna be my driver. I assume you can drive a car."

"Yes sir. But there's a problem with this car."

He frowned. "What?"

"The steering wheel is on the wrong side."

He shook his head. "Americans. Follow me."

I fell in behind Mr. Cole. He led me to the cars at the back of the line. Several men were busy loading equipment into one of the bigger vehicles. Mr. Cole told me to pitch in. He left, going up and down the line shouting orders.

There were big and small boxes to be loaded. Ammunition and guns. Big guns. The only thing I knew about guns came from reading books. These were high-powered, large caliber rifles used only for hunting big game like lions and elephants. Was this a hunting safari? I wanted no part in the killing of any wild animals for trophies. But here I was, maybe a contributing party to the slaughter. I should have walked away, refused to have any part in it. That took courage. As H. Rider Haggard said in *King Solomon's Mines*, fortune favors the courageous. I didn't feel too courageous. I pitched in and did my job. I knew I would regret it.

I had just loaded a box of ammunition onto a truck when I turned to see the young girl from the train. She stood outside one of the Rovers staring at me. I smiled and started to say something. I was interrupted when her mother came barreling out of the Rover shouting at me. A second later, Mr. Cole came running to the scene. He confronted her.

"What the hell's going on, Capi?"

The girl's mother pointed an accusing finger in my direction.

"What is that little bastard doing here?"

Mr. Cole said, "What's the problem?"

She motioned for Mr. Cole to come closer. Took him aside, started gesturing wildly, talking fast in low voice. I couldn't tell what she was saying. She kept glancing and pointing at me, obviously objecting to my presence. When she finished, Cole came marching over. He got in my face.

"What the hell happened with Mrs. Lewis' daughter?"

"Mrs. who?" I asked.

He nodded toward the girl's mother. "Capi Lewis. The girl's mother."

"Nothing happened. The girl and I were just talking in the lobby last night when her mother attacked me."

Mr. Cole said, "She told me she saw you on the train having dinner with some shady characters."

I figured she meant Harry and company.

"I didn't know them. I'd just met them on the train."

"Never mind. Just do your job and stay away from her and Jama."

"Who's Jama?"

"Her daughter, you wanker." He backed off, frustrated. "She wants me to fire you. And if you were anyone else..."

"What does that mean?"

"Forget it. Just stay the hell away from her and her daughter." He punched my chest with his finger. "Understand?"

"Don't worry about that. I don't want to be hit anymore."

Mr. Cole chewed his lip, thinking.

"Are you sure you didn't know those guys on the train?"

"How could I? I've only been here a couple of days. I don't know anyone."

He turned around and headed to Mrs. Lewis. She remained standing by the Rover with her arms around her daughter, a scowl on her face. He took the mother aside again, out of her daughter's hearing. They talked for a minute. She listened. The anger in her face softened. She still gave me a suspicious look but nodded like she agreed with whatever Mr. Cole told her. The woman went to her daughter and said something. They got in their Rover. Mr. Cole came back to me.

"Okay, kid. I told her you'd only been in the country a couple of days and you probably didn't know those guys. So, just let it go. I don't want any trouble on my safari."

"What was shady about those guys on the train?" I asked.

Cole looked at his watch. "Dammit, I don't have time for this shit." He shook his head. "Look. If you have to know, those guys on the train were known poachers and she thought you were in with them."

"So, that's why she called me a poaching bastard. I told her she was mistaken."

"She's got a thing about poachers. She was married to a Brit who got mixed up with some people in that line of work. He ended up getting killed in a poaching raid. Nasty business."

I said to Mr. Cole, "Did you mention my father to her?"

"No," Mr. Cole said. "Why would I?"

"I just wondered if she knew him. Maybe she knows where he is."

Mr. Cole grabbed me by the arm. His grip cut off the circulation.

"You need to stop asking questions? You hear me?"

"Okay, okay," I said.

I pulled away.

He calmed down.

"We need to get on the road," he said.

We headed toward the lead car. He shouted to the line of Land Rovers. "Okay, everyone. Mount up."

The porters, gunbearers, drivers jumped in their cars. The ones who appeared to be guests, like Jama and Capi, took their places in their Rovers. When we reached the lead Rover, Mr. Cole took the passenger side, me in the driver's seat.

Mr. Cole said, "You know how to start this?"

I put my foot on the clutch and the brake. Turned the key. The motor turned over. I gunned it, looked at Mr. Cole.

"Nothing to it," I said.

He waved us forward.

I said, "Before we get started, one more question."

"I told you to stop asking questions."

"Just tell me. Do you know where my father is?"

He shot me a wicked look.

"Drive."

22.

AS WE DROVE, MR. Cole told me who the guests were on the safari. Mr. and Mrs. Singh from India, Mr. Clyde Norris and his fifteen-year-old son, Austin, from Texas, and Mrs. Lewis and her daughter, Jama. The Singhs rode in the second car behind the lead car. Behind them, Mr. Norris and son. Mrs. Lewis and Jama, in the third car behind us. The two Rovers on the end were packed with equipment.

We headed for a town called Kijabe about sixty miles north of Nairobi. We drove through forests of dense trees and across green grasslands. The six Land Rovers rumbled over rutted roads, tires slipping in and out of the muddy grooves cut by years of vehicles. The steering wheel shook so hard my teeth rattled. I kept glancing at the vast herds of wildebeest and zebra blanketing the grasslands. Buzzards lurked on acacia trees waiting for lions to finish feasting on their kill of the day. The highlight of my day was when we stopped and let a herd of elephants cross the road.

There were ten of them. Five females, three young males and two calves. All the guests, including me, jumped out of their cars to witness the passing of these magnificent animals. To observe them up close in the wild was the thrill of my life. They moved with the grace and dignity of creatures that seemed to know they were the superior species on earth. They didn't even bother looking our way.

We made good time considering the condition of the roads. Mostly tire tracks carved out of dirt. I averaged about 30 miles an hour.

Around noon, Mr. Cole ordered me to pull into a clearing covered with trees. It looked like others had stopped there. Mr. Cole said it had been a favorite safari camping ground for years.

The porters bailed out of their Rovers, hurrying to set up for lunch. The lunch table was placed beneath the shade of a tree. Clean linen covered the tables. China and silverware along with glasses, napkins, the full treatment. Boxes full of sliced game meat, bread, ham and other specialty foods from Nairobi shops. Ennis ordered me to set up wooden chairs.

With lunch ready, the guests left their Rovers to take their place at the table. January in Kenya meant a nice, warm day, 23 degrees Celsius. In Virginia, it was winter with temperatures near freezing. I had to deal with all these changes. Temperature, customs, accents. I'd only been in Africa three days, and I had already picked up a slight British accent. Mix that with my Southern accent and I thought it had a sort of backwoods charm. Cole thought it made me sound stupid.

Once the guests were seated, three servers dressed in starched white uniforms served breakfast. First, the ladies, the men on opposite sides. At the head of the table, Mr. Cole.

Ennis motioned for me to follow him to one of the equipment cars. The back gate was lowered. Four porters sat on chairs eating sandwiches and drinking coffee from crude cups. Ennis told me I was to take lunch with the porters. One of the porters pointed to a tray of sandwiches. I grabbed one. It was meat wrapped in thin bread, the same bread I'd seen at the Mombasa market. They noticed my confusion. The porters started talking to each other in what I later learned was the language of the Maasai called Maa. One of them finally spoke to me. He said, "Chapati." They all laughed.

"What?"

"The bread. It's called chapati," one of them said.

"You speak English," I said.

"It is an English country."

I nodded. "Of course."

I examined the sandwich. "What kind of meat is this?"

The porter glanced at his friends. A brief smile, then deadly serious.

"Monkey ass."

I flinched. Held the sandwich at arm's length. "What?"

"Meat from a monkey's ass. Very good."

The four porters stopped eating to watch me. I frowned. Held the sandwich between thumb and middle finger like I was holding a dog turd.

"Ugh." I laid the sandwich on a nearby chair. "Sorry. Don't mean to insult you. But I don't think I want to be eating monkey ass."

Offended silence. Angry glares. I shifted uncomfortably, not knowing what to do. Then the outburst. Rollicking laughter. One porter laughed so hard he spilled his coffee. Knee-slapping roars so raucous the nearby lunch party stopped their civilized discussion to look. Mr. Cole stood, staring. He motioned to Baako. Baako only had to raise an arm and the porters quieted down.

I'd been had.

"Monkey ass?" I said.

The head porter shrugged.

I picked up my abandoned sandwich. Closely examined the meat.

"This looks like ham to me," I said.

"Yes," the porter said, "Ham ass."

A new round of laughter. I joined in the joke. It was their way of welcoming me into the world of Maasai humor. My first friends in Africa turned out to be not British but Africans. It was a sign of things to come.

We ate lunch discussing all sorts of things. They were all Maasai. The leader of the group, Leebo, asked me where I was from. I told him about the United States. They asked a lot of questions about my life in America.

When I told them I'd worked in a zoo, Leebo asked, "What kind of animals are in this zoo?"

I told him it was full of animals from all over the world. I asked Leebo, "Do you have zoos here in Kenya?"

He laughed. "Yes. The whole country is a zoo."

23.

WITH LUNCH OVER, THE porters and kitchen crew cleared the tables. They started setting up camp. I was about to pitch in and help when Mr. Cole came over.

"Hey, kid. Leave that to the porters. Follow me."

He headed for the line of Rovers, stopping at the equipment car. He grabbed a rifle and threw it at me. Luckily, I caught it.

"What's this for?"

"You're going hunting."

"Me?"

"Yeah, you. Grab some ammo and meet me at the car."

It was the first time in my life I'd held a gun. My porter friend, Leebo, noticed how awkward I must have appeared holding the rifle.

"You never shot a rifle?" he asked.

I shook my head. He took the gun from me.

"It is a .260 Winchester. An American gun for an American boy."

"What are we going to shoot?"

The porter shrugged.

"Boss will show you. He's taking the Indian, the white man and his boy on the hunt."

"We're going on a hunt?"

"Yes, that's what we do on a safari."

"We're not going to shoot elephants, are we?"

He grinned. "No, no. Elephant laugh at this gun."

"Why?"

"You need big gun for an elephant. Don't worry. This gun is not for elephant."

"What's it for?"

"Lions."

I swallowed. Hard.

"Don't lions charge you?"

"Only if they're hungry."

The porter grabbed a box of ammunition. Handed it to me. I stared at it not knowing how to load the rifle. The porter took the gun, pulled back the bolt and loaded it. Pushed the bolt forward. He took time to show me how to load it, use the safety, how to aim.

"Very easy," he said.

The rest of the afternoon meant the chores of completing camp setup. The crew finished assembling the tents, moving gear, making sure all the comforts of camp life were in place. Mr. Cole and the two male guests spent their morning getting gear ready for our afternoon outing. Cleaning rifles, checking ammo, discussing the coming hunt. I hung around the men listening to Mr. Cole tell hunting stories. One story he told seemed almost too far-fetched to believe. Mr. Singh, Mr. Norris and Austin pulled their chairs close to listen. I hovered behind Cole to take it all in.

Cole said it was years ago when he first started hiring on as a professional guide and hunter. The clients only wanted one thing---a trophy to take home for bragging rights to their buddies. On this one hunt, he had two clients who had never fired a round at anything bigger than a rabbit. He had outfitted them with a .470 Double Rigby and a Wesley .350 Rigby Mauser. I asked him if they were for killing elephants. He ignored me.

Cole told how he had taken these two gentlemen into a woodland and, as they were walking, they came upon a bull elephant. He wasn't sure if the animal had seen them. They were hidden from the bull by a dense thicket. It was busy chewing on the leaves of a bushwillow tree. I asked Mr. Cole what a bushwillow tree looked like. He ignored me. Then, Mr. Norris from Texas said he wanted to know what a bushwillow tree looked like. Mr. Cole took a good two minutes explaining everything Mr. Norris would ever want to know about a bushwillow tree. Paying customers get all the attention.

When he finished with the bushwillows, Mr. Cole picked up where he left off on the elephant story. He had advised his two clients to move away quietly from the bull. It wasn't a good idea to be that close to a bull and surprise him. No sooner than he told them to move away quietly, one of the clients sneezed. The client politely apologized, but it was too late. The big bull turned on them. It crashed through the thicket, headed for the sneezer. Mr. Cole acted quickly, shouldering his .350 double-barrel Express. He squeezed off one round, then another. The rounds hit solid, the first in the chest, the second high on the forehead. It didn't faze the big bull.

The animal smashed through the thicket in a full charge. The two clients dropped their rifles and ran like hell. One ran free, but the second wasn't as lucky. Before Mr. Cole could reload two new rounds, the bull seized the man with his trunk. Cole said this client weighed over three hundred pounds. He could've been twice that weight and it wouldn't have mattered to the bull. The elephant lifted the man as if he were a bag of beans, shook him so hard the man's false teeth flew out of his mouth. Then the beast impaled the poor fellow on its tusk, spearing him through his chest. Blood and guts spilled on the ground as the elephant wrenched the body from its tusk. The behemoth (Mr. Cole's word) wrapped its trunk around the poor man, wound up like it was going to throw a football and hurled the corpulent (his word again) body a good twenty yards into a bush of thorns.

I interrupted, asking Mr. Cole if he was referring to American or Rugby football. He told me to shut up.

Mr. Norris and Mr. Singh sat wide-eyed, mouths gaping during Cole's reciting of his tall tale about the elephant and the fat man. Mr. Norris, who had been smoking a cigar, was so engrossed in the story it slipped out of his mouth onto the ground. It landed in a clump of leaves and started a small fire. He immediately stamped out the flames, picked up the now partially scorched cigar, brushed it off, and stuck it in his mouth. Cole and Singh gave him a look of disgust. He shrugged, holding the charred remains for Cole and Singh to see. "El Habano." They nodded their approval. The man continued to puff on the smoldering butt.

Off to the side, listening the whole time, Austin stood giggling throughout the horror story.

Mr. Singh asked Cole, "Did you kill the beast?"

Mr. Cole smiled. "Yes, sir. Then I ate him."

Mr. Singh didn't get the humor. Mr. Norris and Austin did. They got a bang out of that one. Mr. Singh reacted with a puzzled smile. He leaned forward and in dead seriousness asked Mr. Cole, "Did you really eat him?"

Mr. Cole said, "The elephant or the client?"

Mr. Singh blushed. He laughed along with us.

Cole headed for the tables. "Time for the hunt."

24.

MR. COLE SUMMONED THE male guests to meet him at the cars. All the men, rifles slung over their shoulders, me included, headed toward the Rovers. On the way, we passed a large umbrella-shaped tree where the porters had strung a white canopy to shade the women. Mrs. Singh, dressed in a fine gown, wearing a wide-brimmed hat and Mrs. Lewis and Jama decked out in women's version of bush clothes, relaxed on canvas lounge chairs. As we were leaving, I glanced at Mrs. Lewis and Jama. Mrs. Lewis was in her chair, eyes closed. Jama was reading a book. When I passed by, she looked up and smiled. I smiled, then ran smack into Mr. Norris, who obviously slowed down to glance at Mrs. Lewis. I apologized to him. He gave me a nasty look. Austin saw the whole thing. He shook his head, shot me a half smile and turned a disgusted frown toward his father.

At the parking area, I headed for the lead car. Mr. Cole stopped me.

"No, kid. You're in the second car with Austin. Ennis will drive you."

Great. Demoted to the kiddie car.

Cole, Singh, Norris and Baako rode in the lead car. Ennis followed closely behind. Me in the back seat beside Austin bouncing around without a word between us. What do you say to a fifteen-year-old boy who wishes he was someplace else?

"So, Austin," I said, "this is all pretty exciting stuff, huh?"

He shrugged. "I missed football for this shit. Whadda you think?"

Our small convoy barreled over a series of dusty roads for hours toward the destination Mr. Cole had in mind. Riding in the second car meant eating the dust of the lead car. Traveling through the African afternoon also meant the various smells of Africa attacking your senses. A mixture of dust and animal dung stirred up by the thousands of creatures parading by.

Animals were everywhere. Gazelle flew by at blinding speed. Herds of wildebeest and zebra stretched along the horizon by the thousands. We even caught sight of several giraffes, their long necks towering above the treetops. And the sounds. Lions roaring, hippos grunting, the drum-like beats of a zebra herd stampede, and wildebeests snorting like geese suffering from colds. Add to that the creepy laughter of hyenas and it had the effect of an out-of-tune orchestra. Then the distant clear trumpet calls of elephants rising above the riot like a fanfare for royalty. I instantly missed my friend Betty. I wondered what she would think of all of this, of her homeland. Maybe she missed it. Looking around, taking in the panorama of animals living free, I swore to myself when I got back home, I would do my best to return Betty to Africa to live the rest of her life in freedom.

The Rovers finally stopped at the edge of a small river. Everyone bailed out. Cole ordered Ennis to stay with the cars. Baako led the way. Mr. Cole carried a double barrel .470 Nitro Express. Mr. Norris, a .427 Westley Richards. His son, Austin, had a .30/06. Mr. Singh, a .350 Mauser rifle. And I had the .260 Winchester. There was enough firepower to start a war.

Baako led us through a stand of trees to an area of open grassland. Mr. Cole huddled with Mr. Norris. Cole called me over and pointed to a rock face not far away.

"Okay, boy, head for those rocks. When you get there, I want you to watch for lions."

"There are lions?"

"What do you think we're doing here? Mr. Norris paid a lot of money to bag a trophy lion. So, watch for them and signal if you see one."

"Why?"

He was getting irritated. "Because I said so."

"So, I'm the bait?"

"Don't flatter yourself, kid."

"How will I signal?"

"Don't yell. That attracts a lion quicker than red meat. Just wave your arms. I'll be watching."

I judged the distance to the rock face. It seemed a mile away.

"What if a lion charges me? I'm not gonna shoot a defenseless animal."

Mr. Cole looked at me as if I were crazy. "Then don't shoot it. It's your funeral."

The biggest danger I ever faced in Virginia were spiders and mosquitoes. They had those in Africa too, only bigger. And now I'm facing lions? With a little old rifle. But I had my legs. I could run. If a lion went after me, I was going to run all the way back to Virginia.

The rock face turned out to be about thirty paces away. I had to sweat through waist-high grass, carefully watching for snakes, lions, other critters. When I reached the rock face, my knuckles were white from gripping the rifle. The rock was about twenty feet tall and as wide as a house. I checked the area for a place where I could climb to safety in case a lion discovered me. There were no visible footholds, but there was a space between the rocks that might protect me in case of attack. But if a lion jumped me from above, I was lunch.

The prospect of being eaten alive, or even dead, caused my heart to pound. I had to control myself. I took the rifle off my shoulder and carefully pushed the safety button to off like Leebo showed me. Now that I had the protection of my rifle, I calmed my breathing to almost normal. If I had to defend against an attack, I wouldn't go without a fight. Or better yet, flight.

I leaned against the rocks, relaxed, ready to meet any challenge. Why am I here, I thought? I just needed a job that didn't involve killing anything. I reminded myself when this safari was over to make a new career choice. Better yet, do what I came here to do, then get the hell out of Africa.

A loud boom instantly followed by the zing of a ricocheting bullet. A spray of rock dust showered down on me. I looked up at the rock face. Just above my head, a fresh hole appeared. Another bang, another blast of rock dust raining on me. One more loud report. A second ricochet. Someone was trying to kill me.

I fell to the ground shouting at the top of my lungs, "Stop shooting."

Silence. I buried my face in African dirt. Dirt never smelled so good.

I heard running, shouting. Mr. Cole was bending over me.

"You okay, kid?"

Joining him, Mr. Norris, Austin, both gawking. I pushed up on one knee trying to catch my breath.

Mr. Norris said, "Son, are you okay?"

I glanced up at the circle of concerned faces. Mr. Norris was visibly shaken. Austin, a silly smile. Mr. Singh finally joined the group, huffing as he ran up to see what had happened.

"Boy, you gave me a scare," Mr. Cole said.

Something phony in Mr. Cole's words. Real insincere. I stood straight, towering over him. I let loose the anger.

"Who was the jackass shooting at me?"

Mr. Cole's words fumbled out of his mouth like lies do. "I thought I saw movement above you in the rocks."

"There was no movement in the rocks," I said.

"Well. What I meant was..." Cole looked at Norris. "Mr. Norris, you saw movement up on the rocks didn't you?"

Norris shook his head. "Austin and I were looking the other way."

Cole turned to Singh. "How about you, Mr. Singh? Did you notice any activity in the direction of Jack?"

Mr. Singh shook his head.

I shouted in Cole's face. "How about asking them if they saw you trying to kill me?"

Mr. Cole couldn't look me in the eye.

"Oh, come on, kid. I swear, there was movement behind you up on the rocks. I thought you were in danger."

"I was. From you trying to kill me."

Norris and Singh exchanged suspicious glances. Baako stood to the side, standing on one leg, emotionless.

Cole was red-faced. "Son, if I wanted to kill you, you'd be dead."

"If you weren't trying to kill me, what were you trying to do?"

"Settle down, okay? Like I said, I thought I saw something up on the rock face. I fired off a few shots to scare it."

I gave him open palms. "To scare what?"

Mr. Cole looked at Baako. "Baako. You saw movement up on the rocks, right?"

Baako stared at Cole, then turned and walked away.

I swallowed bile. My chest heaved. Cole backed off, his head lowered.

"Look, son. Maybe I was mistaken. Maybe there wasn't any movement up on the rocks. Let's forget about all this and go back to camp. Have a nice dinner, a drink, turn in early. Okay? It'll all be forgotten in the morning." He checked the reactions of Norris and Singh. "We're okay?"

Mr. Norris seemed puzzled. Singh shifted uncomfortably. Austin picked his teeth with a piece of grass.

Mr. Cole turned and headed toward the cars. We followed in silence. Before we got to the camp, Austin only said one thing to me.

"That would have been really awesome if he'd killed you."

"Shut up."

He continued picking his teeth.

25.

THE SUN HAD JUST settled on the horizon when we pulled into camp. Behind us dying streaks of sunlight cut through masses of gathering clouds. The reality of the day was giving in to the shadowy world of the African night.

The crew hung lighted kerosene lamps throughout the camp. The kitchen staff was busy setting tables, preparing to serve dinner. I headed for my tent at the edge of the campground. Tired but still upset over almost being shot. Since I met Mr. Cole, too many suspicions, too many unanswered questions. I was so angry I wanted to get the hell out of there, go home, forget Africa. I was almost at my tent when Cole caught up to me.

"Hey, kid. Hold on."

I kept going, shouting at him over my shoulder. "Leave me alone."

Cole grabbed me by the shoulder, swung me around. Facing him, I could see the worry in his eyes.

"Look, kid, you gotta listen to me."

"Stop calling me kid."

His palms went up in surrender.

"Okay. Sorry. I just want to explain what happened."

"I know what happened," I said. "You tried to kill me."

He shook his head. "Why would I want to do that?"

"I don't know," I said. "But when we first met, you weren't the least bit interested in helping me. Then when you found out I was J.A.'s son, you went suddenly weird on me. And I saw you talking to someone on the phone. Was it my father? Then, out of the blue, you offer me a job? Then you try to kill me? You owe me some explanations."

Mr. Cole frowned, scratched his head.

He looked at me with fresh eyes. "Your father said you were a smart kid."

"So, you do know him."

He nodded. "For a long time."

"What's with all the mystery?"

Cole wiped sweat off his face. He was breathing hard.

"Look, I'm not supposed to tell you this, but it's for your own good." He glanced over his shoulder as if being watched. "Right now, your father has this big business deal brewing, and he doesn't have time for you. So, give it a couple of days and maybe he'll get in touch. Okay?"

"Then why did you shoot at me? There was nothing up on the rocks."

He licked his lips. Looked one way then the other, avoiding my stare.

"Okay, you're right. You were never in any danger. But it's not what you think. I wasn't trying to kill you. In the safari business, it's what we call an initiation. Anytime a young man takes a job with a safari they get an initiation into safari life. Today was yours. That's all it was." He withdrew into a thought then gave me a faraway look. "It's the same initiation your father got on his first safari."

I shoved my face at him. "Cut the bullshit. That was no initiation. If you weren't trying to kill me, you were trying to scare the hell out of me to make me go back to America." He blinked. I gave him my squinty eyes. "I think it has something to do with my father and I wanna know what it is."

Cole turned on me with a vengeance. He grabbed my shirt, pulled me toward him. When he barked at me, I could see the fillings in his teeth.

"Look, you little shit. Stop asking questions about your father or you're gonna end up..."

We were nose to nose, staring each other down.

"End up how?" I said.

Cole released his grip. Backed off.

"Look. Your father's a powerful man. Not someone you want to cross."

That took me by surprise.

"Ever since I got here, the mention of his name seems to scare the hell out of everyone. And now you're telling me I need to be afraid him too? Who the hell is he?"

Cole took a deep breath. Something bad was churning inside him. He spoke with clenched teeth. "I've said too much already."

Mr. Norris appeared.

"Is everything okay here?"

Our argument had caught the attention of the others. I looked past him. Mrs. Lewis and her daughter were staring.

Cole smiled. "Not to worry, sir. I was just apologizing to Jack about the unfortunate accident this afternoon."

Norris turned from me to Cole with obvious concern.

"Well, I hope all is okay."

Cole said, "Yes, all is fine, sir." Cole turned to me. "Jack, now that we've worked that out, I want to invite you for dinner. We'll have a relaxing evening and I'm sure we'll end up laughing about all of this."

What's the old expression? If looks could kill? He was lucky they can't.

"If you don't mind, sir, I'll pass," I said.

I walked away.

My tent had been set up at the edge of the campground. I crawled in and closed the flap. A small cot pushed against the walls. I threw my pack on the ground and fell face down on the narrow camp bed. I tried to sleep, but Mr. Cole's words kept spinning in my mind. I remembered a warning from my mother. You stick your nose in other people's business you'll get it cut off. What was my father's business? I planned to keep the nose I had. But I wasn't going to wait for long.

Sleep finally came.

A couple of hours later, the murmur of voices, laughter, sounds of silverware on plates, glass against glass woke me. At a distance, animal sounds. The grunt of lions. An elephant trumpeting. Crickets buzzing and clicking. I stared at the roof of the canvas tent for a while before dozing off. I woke up a second time to the soft crunch of footsteps coming close outside.

"Mr. Sims?"

A woman's voice. I sat up.

The voice again. "Mr. Sims? Are you awake?"

I rubbed the sleep away. Opened the tent flap. Standing there, Mrs. Lewis' daughter, Jama. She had on an evening gown, makeup, her hair brushed back. More beautiful than I remembered. She bent over, peering into my tent. In her hands, a plate full of food.

"Hi," I said.

She waited. Smiled.

"Oh," I said, "Would you like to come in?"

"Yes. Thank you."

I opened the flap to give her room to enter. She handed me the food plate. I took it and put it on the cot. I held the tent flap open. Like the lady she was, she lifted her dress just so high, bent down, and moved gracefully into my makeshift home. She stood while I closed the entry way. She waited. Looked at me. Stupid me.

"My manners. Did you want to sit?"

She nodded. I put the plate of food on my lap, brushed off the blanket. She sat, hands folded in her lap. An awkward silence. She held out her hand.

"I'm Jama."

"Yes, I know. You're Mrs. Lewis' daughter."

I shook the daintiest hand I'd ever seen. She withdrew, smiling, sort of blushing.

"And you are Mr. Sims."

"Jack."

"Okay, Jack," she said.

I was taken with her face, skin like pure ivory carved into features that made me want to look forever.

"By the way. My mother wants you to know how sorry she is about attacking you. She's been overly protective of me since my father died."

Another awkward silence. I smiled at her. She smiled. I thought I'd try to say something intelligent.

"You hear that? The clicking sounds?"

She nodded.

I said, "I love the sound of crickets. It makes me feel at home."

She said, "Those are not crickets. They're cicadas."

"Oh, right. We've got those back home too."

Another smile. Then she did something that caused my heart to skip a beat. She put her hand on mine.

"I hope my mother didn't hurt you too much."

I shrugged. "Nah. It was nothing."

She laughed. Coughed a little. Then frowned.

"I heard about what happened today on the hunt," she said. "Mr. Norris was talking about it at dinner."

"Mr. Cole nearly shot me."

Her mouth turned up. Such a perfect mouth.

"How did that happen?"

I wanted to tell her why I thought Cole shot at me. But I honored Cole's advice to leave it alone.

"It was an accident," I said.

She leaned forward, elbows on her knees.

"Hmm. An accident? That doesn't sound like Mr. Cole."

"You know him?"

"He and my father were in business together. They had a safari company. Cole and Lewis Safaris." Her mood went melancholy. "They were good friends." She smiled at me, eyes fluttering.

"What happened to their company?"

"I don't know. I was pretty young at the time. There was a lot of talk. Something about ivory and poaching. I remember Mr. Cole coming to the house one night. He and my father in the den, shouting at each other. I was only sixteen. Then Mr. Cole left the company. A year later my father was dead."

"I'm sorry," I said. An awkward silence. "How did he die?"

Jama took a deep breath. "It was reported as an accident, but we think someone had him killed."

"That's awful," I said. Who killed him?"

"The man my mother thinks was responsible has a reputation for operating one of the major poaching enterprises in Africa. Word is he's made a fortune killing thousands of elephants for their ivory. He's ruthless. Anyone who stands in his way..."

She shook her head.

"So, why don't they arrest the guy?"

"He's like a ghost. Nobody's been able to find him."

"Who is he?" I asked.

She turned to face me, her eyes squinting, her face red. "He's a monster. I hope he burns in hell." The veins in her neck went tense with anger. "His name is J.A. Quill."

Her words caught in my throat like a bone. I choked, coughing my lungs out. I grabbed the water she brought with my dinner and drank it in one quick gulp. Jama patted my back until I recovered.

"Are you okay?" she said, her face wrinkled with concern.

I finally settled down. I swallowed hard, nodded.

"I'm good," I lied, still trying to catch my breath.

Jama stared at me, her hand on her chest.

"Did I say something to upset you?"

That was my cue to confess about my father. But now was not the time.

"No, no," I said, "I just got something caught in my throat."

We sat in silence while I recovered. She kept rubbing my back. I felt her staring, but I didn't dare look her in the eye for fear she would see right through me. I tried to process what she had said. My father, a poacher and a murderer? No. Unimaginable. Incomprehensible. It couldn't be. But the evidence was mounting against him. The man I grew up worshiping was a hard-working, honest man. Sure, he'd left me and my mother destitute. That was bad. But it was a far cry from becoming a poacher or a murderer. This was a man who taught me a lot about animals. I watched how gentle he was with them. He had introduced me to Betty, beautiful Betty, the elephant he cared for, the animal that had become my friend. To imagine him being the mastermind behind the slaughter of elephants like Betty for their ivory made no sense. But to be a poacher and a murderer. Poachers and murderers don't read stories to their kids at night, don't take them to baseball games or play catch with them, and they don't take them to the zoo. If it were all true, what had happened to change him? I tried to sort it out. To comprehend the impossible. It was like trying to imagine where space ends. A question with no answer. I was more determined than ever to find my father.

I considered my next move. I didn't want to lie to Jama, but to tell her it was my dad who might have killed her father would have been the end of whatever relationship we had. But if I ever had a chance with her, it was best to start by being honest.

I sat up straight, trying to gather the strength to tell her the truth. I took her hands in mine --- God, they were beautiful hands --- and I was about to tell her who I actually was when she interrupted me.

"By the way," she said, her voice hushed, urgent, "earlier tonight something happened between my mother and Mr. Cole that didn't make sense."

I've read about divine providence, but the change in subject couldn't have come at a better time.

"What happened?"

"Well," she said, "after everyone turned in for the night, I was awakened by the sound of my mother's voice. It was coming from Mr. Cole's tent which is right next to mine. Mr. Cole and my mother were arguing."

"What about?"

"Mr. Cole told my mother he was taking Mr. Norris on a hunt tomorrow and he didn't think it was safe for me and her to go along. Mother reminded him she had grown up in Kenya, going on hunts all her life. She asked what was different about this one? He told her he was in charge and his decision was final. That's when she asked if it had anything to do with J.A. Quill."

"The poacher?" I asked, feeling uncomfortable at the mention of my father.

"Yes," she said.

"Why would she bring that up?"

"I don't know. Probably something to do with her job."

"What's her job?"

"She works for the Kenyan Wildlife Service in the anti-poaching division." Jama paused as if to consider what to say next. "Mr. Cole got real angry, shouting at her. He stormed out of the tent, telling her if she was going on the hunt to stay the hell out of his way."

"So, the mention of this Quill guy made him change his mind?"

"Apparently."

"Do you think Cole has anything to do with Quill?"

I felt strange referring to my father by his last name. The gap between us was growing.

She shrugged. "I don't know. But for some reason, my mother seems to think so."

A second later, Jama's mother called for her. Jama grabbed my face and pulled me to her. Her kiss was as warm as a summer breeze. She stood.

"I've got to go." She shouted to her mother, "I'm coming."

She left the tent in a hurry.

I stood up too fast. Hit my head on the supporting tent pole.

I heard Mrs. Lewis say, "Is everything okay?"

"Yes," Jama said.

Her mother's voice didn't sound concerned. Then the tent flap opened. It was Mrs. Lewis, peering in, smiling.

"Jack, I hope my daughter didn't disturb you."

I almost choked again. "No, ma'am. She was properly not disturbing. I mean we were both properly undisturbed."

Mrs. Lewis laughed. "I'm sure everything was proper. Well, we won't be bothering you anymore tonight. Maybe tomorrow we could visit a bit. I'd like to hear more about what happened on the hunt today."

"Yeah. Yes ma'am. Yes." God, what an idiot. "I mean yes, Mrs. Lewis."

She laughed. "Good night, Mr. Sims. And please, call me Capi."

She closed the flap. I listened as they walked away. I considered what Jama told me about my dad. I knew eventually I would have to reveal to her who I was. That would probably be the end of our relationship. But now with the knowledge of what happened to Jama's father, possibly at the hands of my father, it was no longer a case of my revenge. It was now a case of getting justice for Jama. I wasn't sure I knew the difference.

26.

WE GOT A LATE start the next morning. Mrs. Singh threw a fit at breakfast when she learned her husband was going on the hunt. She wanted to go shopping in Nairobi. Mr. Singh tried to calm her. She wasn't cooperating. Went on a rant, shouting at him.

"You and your dead animals. I hate them all, hanging in that den of yours. It's disgusting. Now you want to shoot another poor creature and stuff him so you can be the big man with your friends."

She said all this while storming to her tent. Eventually, all we could hear was her muffled complaints ending in a pathetic bout of sobbing.

After breakfast, Mr. Singh informed Mr. Cole he was staying behind to comfort his wife. That meant everyone except the Singhs were going on the hunt. All morning, as Cole got us ready, he seemed nervous, especially around Capi. He wouldn't even look at her.

We all piled into two Rovers and hit the road. Cole, Mr. Norris, Baako in the front two seats of the lead Rover, Cole driving. In the second car, Ennis drove with Capi in the front seat, Jama in the middle seat and me stuck in the back with Austin. Mr. Norris had missed a chance at a lion, but Cole told him he knew a place where he would have a shot at a buffalo.

We had camped the night before, south of the village of Kijabe. Leaving camp in the morning, we headed north toward the Aberdare mountains known to be teeming with game like buffalo, lions and elephants. The Rovers took us across fields, through mudholes, ditches, volcanic dust, rocks, and boulders. The landscape proved to be as much of a mixed bag as the roads. We passed through dense forests, climbed mountains, steep-sided ravines, sailed through green pastures and had to cross a couple of rivers. The views were awesome. Waterfalls were everywhere.

Two hours later, the Rovers inched along a dirt road overlooking a vast forested valley below. Capi yelled at Cole to stop.

The cars pulled into a grassy area. Capi climbed out and walked over to Cole's Rover.

Mr. Norris spoke first. "Why are we stopping here?"

Capi said, "I thought you would like to experience one of the many wonders of Kenya."

"Where are we?" Norris asked.

Capi said, "This is the Nyahururu Forest."

"The what?" he asked.

Capi laughed. "Never mind. All you need to know is this is one of the most beautiful places in Africa."

Mr. Norris said, "What is that noise?"

Norris was referring to a distant roar that sounded like a freight train.

Capi said, "It's a spectacular waterfall. You've got to see it, sir."

"Well, let's have a look?" He straightened his hat. "Lead the way, madam."

Mr. Norris followed Capi who headed for a path through a thick stand of trees toward the sound of the waterfall. Cole, Ennis and Baako grabbed their guns, going along to protect their client. But Jama didn't move. She sat still in the Rover, arms crossed, staring ahead. Capi looked back at me and smiled. She whispered something to Mr. Norris. He shouted at Austin to join the group. Before they all disappeared, Austin gave me a goofy smile and a weird thumbs up.

I was about to follow when I noticed Jama wasn't moving. I said, "Don't you want to go with them?"

Jama smiled. "Really, Jack? Could I be more obvious?"

Her lashes slowly lowered then opened like the wings of a butterfly. She left her seat and joined me in the back seat. She put her hand on my shoulder and kissed me. Something was slowly dawning on me.

I squeezed her hand. "Oh, I get it now."

She shook her head. "I wanted to be alone with you. Let's face it. We're on a safari with a lot of older people and a juvenile. You're the only one I have anything in common with. If it weren't for you being here, I'd be going out of my mind."

She looked at me with a quizzical cocked head. "Am I being too forward?" she said.

"No," I said, a little too hurriedly. "You're being perfectly forward." Dammit. When I was around her, my mouth lost connection to my brain. She seemed to get pleasure out of my obvious discomfort.

She broke the ice.

"You know, I knew you were from the United States the first time I saw you on the train."

"Really?"

"It's easy to spot an American. Especially the men."

"How?"

"You all have an attitude unlike anyone else in the world."

"What kind of attitude?" I asked.

"You're so sure of yourselves. So arrogant."

"You think I'm arrogant?"

"Oh, yes, Jack Sims. You are one arrogant American."

I folded my arms. "I don't think that's true."

Again, the butterfly eyelashes.

"It wasn't meant as an insult," she said. "I rather like it. The boys I'm used to are so..." She hesitated. "... British."

"Is that bad?"

"No. It's just that British boys are raised to be..." She put a finger to her lips.

I tried my British accent. "Proper?"

"That's a terrible British accent," she said.

I was so hypnotized by her I didn't notice the stirring in the bush off to our left.

"When I met you in the hotel," she said, "I wish we'd had more time to get to know each other."

"Your mother put a stop to that," I said.

"As I told you, she's very protective."

I laughed. "Yeah. Knocking the shit out of me was pretty protective."

She smiled. "Actually, she thinks you're quite charming."

"She has a physical way of showing it," I said.

Something cracked in the forest next to us. We looked at each other.

I said, "Did you hear that?"

She nodded. We focused on the dense undergrowth. Her eyes widened. We both searched the mass of trees, bushes. Another sound, louder and closer. Rustling leaves. Snapped twigs. Jama held out a hand, trembling.

She whispered. "Get... get your gun."

I scanned the woods. More sounds. A dark shape, quick movements. I could hear my heart beating. Jama's hand was over her mouth. She was clearly frightened. The sound I dreaded came. Low rumbling, snorts, grunts. Then the most piercing trumpet call I've ever heard.

A massive bull elephant crashed through the underbrush into the open field between us. He might as well have been a locomotive.

Jama shouted, "The gun. Get the gun."

The elephant closed ground quickly, kicking up dust, flinging his trunk in the air, ears flapping. I got out of the Rover and faced the giant.

"What are you doing?" Jama screamed.

"Don't panic," I told her.

"I'm getting the gun," she yelled.

Jama hurried to the rear of the car and grabbed a rifle. She threw it to her shoulder and took aim. I grabbed the gun before she could pull the trigger.

"No," I shouted. I tossed the gun aside. Jama fell back into the Rover.

"Are you crazy?" she shouted.

I turned toward the elephant. It stopped only yards from delivering us a crushing blow. I threw my hands in the air and shouted, "Whoa, whoa." I stood my ground, staying as calm as I could. The bull stopped. It seemed confused. It flapped its ears, rocking on its feet. I could hear Jama's breathing, hard and struggling.

I told her in a soft voice, "Don't move."

The animal hesitated, trying to decide if I was friend or foe. He threw his trunk in the air. It became a staring contest between me and the bull. In that moment, I thought of Betty, the gentle giant I had come to know in the Virginia zoo. I remembered how she responded to my voice. Not the words but the way the words were spoken. I had learned elephants listen to the tone in your voice, not your words. They watch your eyes for perceived threats. And they can literally smell danger. This is their only way of knowing how to trust humans.

I continued to hold my arms in the air, palms facing the elephant. I remained calm, speaking softly, looking directly at the big guy. He knew by the look in my eyes, by my expression, by the sound of my voice, by my smell I was no threat.

I heard Jama crying. She spoke, voice shaking. "Make him go away."

"Just be calm," I said, "and everything will be okay."

I stared straight into the elephant's eyes. He returned the look. His tusks were massive. His ears flapped nervously. I nodded, kept talking, low and easy. Told him we meant him no harm. To my astonishment, he huffed a little. Turned, continued watching me. A wild look in his eyes, still uncertain. He blinked. I gave him a gentle pushing motion urging him to leave. He seemed to understand. He backed away. Keeping an eye on me, he quietly turned and disappeared into the woods.

I turned to Jama. She had her face buried in her hands, sobbing.

"It's okay. He's gone," I told her.

She peeked between fingers. Sat up, looked around. Took a deep breath, studied the woods, looking to see if we were safe. Her eyes shifted slowly toward me with a cutting glance. She started toward me, picking up momentum until she bolted at me. She slapped me so hard I felt my neck pop. Then she threw her arms around me, gave me the biggest, wettest kiss I've ever had. We embraced for a long time.

We sat in the Rover for what seemed like hours with Jama's arm around me, her head on my shoulder. When the others returned, Capi got in the Rover, smiling.

She said, "I hope you two had a nice visit."

She winked.

Jama blushed. She gave me a knowing look. "Nice is not exactly the word for it."

Capi's eyebrows raised. She was about to say something but left it alone. I'm glad she did.

27.

WE STILL HAD A safari hunt ahead of us. We headed south. Although I couldn't hear everything he was saying, I could tell Mr. Norris was getting excited about the chance of bagging a rhino. I planned to avoid witnessing that tragedy.

It was tough going for a few miles. The road cut through heavy forests, slipping and sliding over steep twists and turns. At one point, Cole's Rover got temporarily stuck in a mudhole. All the men got out and pushed it free. We drove on until we arrived at a clearing. Waiting was a man in a World War II jeep.

Heavy-set, dressed in typical hunting gear, a pith helmet and highly polished boots.

Cole pulled alongside the jeep. Ennis parked beside Cole. Cole jumped out and immediately went to greet the man. He gave him a military salute, holding it until the stranger returned it. They talked for a minute. Couldn't hear what they were saying. Cole and the stranger kept shooting suspicious glances at the rest of us. I could tell Capi was losing patience with this private conversation. At one point, the man raised his voice to Cole. When Cole threw up his hands in surrender, I got out of the Rover and approached Cole and the stranger.

"What's going on?" I asked.

"Get back in the car, kid," Cole said.

"Who are you, sir?" I asked the man.

Cole answered, teeth clenched. "I said get back in the car."

I shrugged. Started to my car. Capi got out of her Rover, arms folded, a scowl on her face. She approached Cole and the stranger.

"Would you please introduce me?" she said to Cole.

Cole got nervous.

"Capi, this is Mr. Mason. He's an old friend from our army days."

I recalled in Cole's office, Cole mentioning something to Ennis about having some business with a guy named Mason.

Capi looked from Mason to Cole. "Are you forgetting something, Phillip?"

Cole's eyes shut, his head nodding nervously. He said, "This is Capi Lewis."

Mason simply nodded.

Capi's eyes narrowed. "Mr. Mason, what are you doing out here in the middle of nowhere?"

Cole came between Capi and Mason. "That's none of your business, Capi."

Capi pointed an accusing finger at Cole. "I'm making it my business, Phillip." She turned to Mason who gave her a cold, hard look. "So, Mr. Mason, what the hell business do you have with Mr. Cole?"

Mason glared at her, then cut his eyes to Cole. Cole shifted, nervous as hell.

"Capi, it's alright. As I said, Mason and I are old friends. I just asked him to meet me here to discuss some personal business. It's nothing you need to worry about. Okay?"

Capi's arms were still folded. She wasn't budging. Neither was Mason. They locked eyes for a moment. Without a word, Mason grabbed a rifle from the jeep. He jumped out and started marching across the open field toward a stand of thick trees and undergrowth. Cole gave Capi a weak smile. He hurried to his Rover, took his double barrel .470 Nitro Express and took off after Mason. Baako started to follow Cole.

"You stay here, Baako."

Capi snapped at Cole. "What the hell are you doing, Phillip?"

Cole stopped, not looking at Capi.

"Won't take long, Capi," he said. His words were clipped.

Capi yelled after Cole. "Did you forget Mr. Norris?"

Cole ran after Mason like a kid trying to catch up to a parent.

Capi cupped her hands around her mouth and yelled, "Cole?"

The two men disappeared into the thicket.

"What's going on?" Mr. Norris asked.

Capi turned to Ennis. "Do you know this Mason fellow?" she asked.

Ennis shook his head. Smoothed his moustache.

Capi turned to Baako. "Shouldn't you be going with him, Baako?"

As usual, Baako said nothing.

We waited. Capi paced. Checked her watch. A fast-traveling black cloud overtook us. Dropped a shower of rain, then moved on. I got in the Rover. Jama and I glanced at each other. She seemed as confused as I was.

Capi finally had enough of waiting. She went to the back of a Rover, grabbed a rifle.

Jama stood up in the Rover. "Mother, what are you doing?"

"I don't like what's going on here. I'm going to find out who this Mason fellow is and why he's here." Capi turned to Baako. "Baako, follow me."

Capi started toward Cole and Mason. Baako didn't budge. Ennis jumped from his car, overtook Capi and blocked her way.

"Sorry, Mrs. Lewis, I can't let you do this."

Capi brought the rifle around, trigger on the trigger finger.

"Get out of my way," she snapped.

Ennis stood his ground. "No, Mrs. Lewis. You're a guest here and you have no right to interfere with Mr. Cole."

"I demand to know who this Mason fellow is and what he's up to."

"Sorry ma'am, but that's none of your business."

Capi pushed toward Ennis. "Do you know who I am?"

"Yes ma'am."

"Then you know this meeting between Cole and this Mason fellow might well be a government matter."

"I don't know anything about that. I just know Mr. Cole told me not to let anyone interfere with this meeting today."

"Do you know what it's about?"

"No ma'am. I only work here."

Mr. Norris finally had enough of waiting. He jumped out of his car and confronted Ennis, saying, "Look, Mr... What's your name again?"

"Ennis."

"I don't know what the hell is going on here and I don't care. I paid a lot of money to get me a lion. That didn't happen so Cole promised me a rhino. And I'm not leaving here until I get what I paid for. I only have a few more days before we go back home, and I don't..."

The sharp crack of a rifle turned our attention to the woods.

Capi said, "What the hell?"

Ennis looked at Baako. They moved quickly. Baako threw a rifle at Ennis, grabbed another weapon. They took off running in the direction of the gunshot. Capi started to follow, rifle in hand but Jama grabbed her arm.

"Mother, you're scaring me. Please don't go."

Capi put the rifle back in the truck and put her arm around Jama. We waited.

It didn't take long before they returned, Mr. Mason leading the way. Ennis carried Baako's gun. Baako held a limp Phillip in his arms, hurrying toward the cars. Cole was groaning, his shirt soaked in blood. We all bailed out of the cars.

"What the hell happened?" Capi asked.

Mason snapped at Baako. "Put him in my car. I'll get him to Nairobi."

Baako carefully laid Cole in the back of Mason's jeep. Mason jumped in the driver's seat, started the motor. Capi cornered him.

"I asked you a question. What happened?"

"Cole got between me and a rhino. I took the shot before I saw Cole. It was an accident."

"What rhino?" Capi barked. "I didn't hear any rhino."

"Get away from the jeep," Mason shouted. "I need to get him to a hospital."

"You're lying," Capi yelled. "This has something to do with J.A. He put you up to this, didn't he?"

Mason threw the jeep into gear. "Get the hell out of the way," he snapped.

Capi ran to Cole's side. I was right behind her. There was a dark hole in Cole's chest, blood pooling in the jeep bed. His eyes rolled back in his head.

Capi yelled to Mason. "Don't you move."

Mason yelled, "Get out of the way, ma'am."

Capi ignored him, leaning over Cole. Everyone backed off letting Capi do what she could to help Cole. Capi unbuttoned Cole's shirt, examined the wound. She felt his neck for a pulse.

She shouted at Mason. "He won't make it to Nairobi. There's a hospital in Nyeri, just north of here."

"Get out of the way or I'll run you over," Mason shouted. He threw the jeep into reverse.

Capi wasn't moving. Cole grabbed her shirt and pulled her close to him. She hovered over him as he whispered something in her ear. I couldn't hear what he was saying. She listened, a frown on her face. When Cole finally collapsed, letting go of Capi, her eyes cut toward me. It was the same look in her eyes when she attacked me in the hotel.

Cole's head fell to one side.

Without warning, Mason gunned the jeep. The jeep's wheels spun, got traction, taking off south like a rocket. He was out of sight before anyone could react.

Capi ran toward the lead Rover. Jumped in the driver's seat about to start the car. Ennis rushed over, grabbed the keys and pocketed them.

Capi was furious. "Give me those keys."

"Can't do that, ma'am."

"That bastard's not taking Cole to a hospital," she said. "He's going to let him die."

"I'm sorry, but I have clients here and their safety comes first."

Capi screamed in frustration. Jumped out of the lead Rover, hurried toward me and smashed me in the face so hard I went down. Nearly blacked out. I heard shouting.

"Mother. What are you doing? Are you crazy?"

Capi yelled, "Baako, get him up."

My eyes opened. Blurry. I saw Baako walk away.

Capi screamed. "Where are you going, Baako?" She turned to Ennis, shouting orders. "Ennis. Get him up. Tie his hands."

Jama pleaded. "Stop it, Mother. Stop it."

Ennis stood his ground. "Ma'am, I don't take orders from you."

Capi grabbed Ennis by the shirt. She shouted, "You know who I work for and if you don't think I can have you arrested when we get to Nairobi, just try me."

Ennis backed off. Capi released her grip.

She shouted, "Give me the goddamned keys to the Rover."

"Okay, but you won't be able to catch Mason now. He's long gone."

"Forget Mason. I'll deal with him later." She nodded toward me. "Right now, I need to get this bastard in camp to question him. It's a government matter, and you had better cooperate."

Ennis gave her the keys.

"Find something to tie his hands and get him in the truck."

Ennis disappeared from my view. I shook my head. Tried to clear it. I sat up. Ennis returned, pulling me to my feet.

"Capi," I shouted, "what the hell is going on here?"

Capi pushed her face to within inches of mine.

"Shut up!" Capi turned to Jama. "Get in the truck."

Jama hurried into the Rover. Ennis wrapped a cord around my wrists. He pushed me into the truck behind Capi. Jama was at my side, her arm around me, crying.

Mr. Norris was confused. Austin's mouth gaped.

"What are you doing, ma'am?" Mr. Norris said.

Capi spoke in a calm voice. "Sorry, Mr. Norris, this is now government business. Ennis will make sure you and your son get back to camp." Capi turned to Jama. Jama was in tears. "You go with them."

Jama jumped in the car with me.

"No, I'm going with you."

Capi didn't argue. She gunned the Rover and we took off.

28.

"WHERE IS HE?" CAPI shouted at me as she drove.

"Where is who?" I shouted.

"You know who," she shrieked. "Where is your father?"

"What does my father have to do with you?"

"Don't play games with me. You know why I'm asking."

I shook my head. "I don't."

Jama shouted, "Mother, stop it. You're acting crazy."

"Stay out of this, Jama."

Capi was speeding so fast over bumpy roads the Rover kept going airborne. Every time it came crashing to earth, the ropes tying my hands cut deeper. Jama had her arm around me, trying her best to comfort me.

"Are you okay?" she said. There was genuine concern in her voice. "I'm so sorry," she said. "I don't know what's gotten into her," she said.

I tried to speak, but my jaw was sore. All the way to camp, Jama begged her mother to explain herself. Capi ignored her. Jama started crying. Gave me those big eyes. She kept saying how sorry she was. I could only nod, trying to nurse some feeling into my face.

By the time we got to camp, it was dark. Capi dragged me out of the Rover. She marched me into her tent. She told Jama to stay out. My hands were on fire from the ropes on my wrists. She forced me into a chair. Bent over me, finger pointing, teeth gritted.

"I will ask you one more time. Where is he?"

She gripped my collar so tight I choked.

"I really don't know what you're talking about."

Capi pulled tight on my collar. "Admit it. You are J.A. Quill's son. And you know how to find him, don't you?"

It all came clear. Cole must have told Capi who I was when he was in Mason's jeep. Capi tightened her grip on my collar. I was choking. I swear there was smoke coming out of her nostrils.

"Yeah, I am J.A. Quill's son," I said. "But I swear I don't know where he is."

She released her grip. It took me a moment to catch my breath.

Capi took a chair and faced me. She studied me a moment. "Why didn't you tell us who you were?"

I took a deep breath. Now that the truth was out, I was relieved. But I dreaded Jama finding out who I was.

I said, "Before I explain, could you please untie my hands?"

Capi pulled up a chair facing me. Studied me for a moment. Untied my hands. Leaned back and said, "Okay, I'm listening."

I went into the whole story about the fight with an ivory broker in Mombasa. The kidnapping by David Newman. Kicked off the train. The Mau Mau guy who spared my life. All about me being the son of J.A. Quill. "

"Now, you're giving me grief about it," I said. "That's why I didn't tell you. I'm tired of being J.A. Quill's son."

Capi considered what I'd told her. She shook her head.

"That still doesn't answer my question. Where is your father?"

"Look, Capi, you've got to believe me, I don't know."

She went nose to nose with me.

"I don't believe you."

A timid voice came from outside the tent. It was Jama.

"Mother, what is going on in there?"

"Get to your tent, Jama."

Capi, to me. "Where's your father's headquarters?"

"His what?"

She started pacing. "When Cole was in Mason's jeep, I asked him where J.A. was. He told me you were J.A.'s son, and you probably knew where your father was located."

I saw Jama slip quietly into the tent.

I jumped out of my chair. "He was lying," I said.

Capi pushed me back into the chair.

"Why would Cole lie when he knew he was near death," Capi said. "Dying men don't lie, Jack."

"What's that," I said, "some kind of dying rule?"

She put her hand on my shoulder and squeezed. Her eyes narrowed. She spoke softly.

"Why should I then be false, since it is true that I must die here and live hence by truth?"

I mimicked her slitted eyes. "What does that mean?"

She pulled back, shaking her head.

"It's Shakespeare, Jack. It means dying men don't lie."

"I'm more of a Hemingway man," I said.

She shook he head. "The point is, Cole had no reason to lie. So, for the last time, where is your father?"

"If I tell you the truth, will you stop hitting me?"

"Yes," she said, perking up, "I promise."

"Then here's the truth and nothing but the truth," I said. "I DON'T KNOW."

She hit me. I felt blood trickle down the side of my mouth.

"Jack, I'm going to get the truth out of you if I have to..."

Jama came charging in.

"Stop it, Mother. That's enough."

Jama put herself between me and Capi.

"Get out of the way, Jama."

"No," Jama said. "You have to hit me before you hit him again."

When Jama came to my defense, it stunned Capi. It was like Jama had punched her mother in the stomach. Capi backed away. Her mouth twisted in doubt.

"All right, Jama. You made your point. Now, get out of the way."

Jama shook a finger at her mother. "No more hitting."

Capi nodded. Jama moved away. She didn't leave.

Capi looked at me with fresh eyes. She pulled up a chair and sat, leaning forward, elbows on her knees, fingers locked.

"All right. Let me try another way." She smiled and spoke to me as if we were best friends. "What did you tell Cole about your father's whereabouts?"

"What is so important to everyone about where my father is?"

She lowered her voice. "Until I can trust you, that remains on a need-to-know basis."

"It's something to do with you working for the government. Right?"

"Just tell me what you told Cole about your father's whereabouts and I'll leave you alone," Capi said.

"Look. I've been wondering where he was since I was twelve years old. That's why I'm here. To find the bastard and make him pay."

Capi was confused. "Pay for what?"

"For breaking my mother's heart," I said.

Capi stood, circled me twice. She stopped and stared at me. Again, a look like she'd never laid eyes on me.

"You really don't know where he is, do you?"

"That's what I've been trying to tell you. I wish the hell I did. And dammit, I'm not going to say another word until you tell me why the hell you want to know where my goddamned father is."

Jama held an open hand to her mother.

"If you don't mind, Mother, I have a few questions to ask Jack."

Jama moved close, arms folded, looking down on me, frowning. I knew what was coming.

"Last night when I told you about J.A. Quill, why didn't you admit he was your father?"

"I tried," I said, "but you interrupted me."

She turned her head in thought, obviously remembering what happened.

"You had more chances after that," she said.

"I know," I said, realizing my voice was cracking. "But I was afraid it would come between us because of what my dad did to your…"

She got the point.

Jama continued. "I'm not angry with you because you didn't admit who you were. I'm angry because you didn't trust me with it." Her emotion took hold. "Did you really think I would blame you for what your father did to my father?"

"Most people would."

"I'm not most people, Jack."

"Okay," I said, "I should have told you. But put yourself in my place. I arrived here a few of days ago, and when I mentioned my father's name to people, it caused nothing but trouble. And now, I find out my father might be a poacher and a murderer. I only thought he was a deadbeat dad. I've been kidnapped, shot at, beaten up, almost killed, accused of lying and then I meet this wonderful girl and because of what my father might have done to her father I'm in danger of losing her..."

I couldn't continue.

Jama faced Capi and said, "Are you satisfied now?"

Capi gave her daughter a closed-mouth smile. She turned to me. "Okay, so you don't know where your father is. And I'm sorry I hit you."

"Yeah," I said, "it's becoming a bad habit."

Capi said, "But you have to admit, I had good reason to doubt you when Cole told me with his dying breath..."

"Would you stop it with the dying stuff? By the way," I said, "Jama told me about your argument with Cole in his tent the other night. And that you work for something called the Kenyan Service."

"Kenyan Wildlife Service," she said. She gave Jama a disapproving look. "My job is with the anti-poaching task force. We heard Cole would be meeting with someone to settle a score. Obviously, that someone turned out to be Mason who I think was sent by your father to kill Cole."

"What score?" I asked.

"Cole wouldn't tell me. He claimed it was a personal matter. Maybe when we get to Nairobi my boss will have some information about that."

Answers were falling into place. "So, that's why you were on this safari?"

She nodded. "Yes. To keep an eye on Cole. Of course, we claimed we were just on vacation. But I think he knew better."

"How long have you been trying to find my father?"

"For years. But based on new information, we believe wherever he is, he might not be there for long."

"Where's he going?" I asked.

"Enough with the questions, Jack," she said.

Capi turned away, rubbing her forehead as if nursing a headache. She glanced at me over her shoulder, giving me a curious look. "God, Jack, I just can't make up my mind about you."

"Well, I'm not too sure about you either," I said.

We all got a laugh out of that one.

By this time, with everything that I had learned, my plan to find my father seemed pretty remote.

"I don't know, Capi. I'm beginning to think I wasted my time coming to Africa."

Capi glanced at her daughter. It was obvious my remark upset Jama. Capi quietly walked away, leaving us alone.

Jama wrapped her arms around me. She settled her eyes on mine, then gave me a long, lingering kiss. "Now do you think you wasted your time coming to Africa?"

I gave her my best smile. "Who said I wasted my time coming to Africa?"

29.

WITH COLE GONE, CAPI took charge of the safari. It was too late to try to reach Nairobi before nightfall. She ordered everyone up by dawn the next day. She wanted to be in Nairobi by early morning. Like all of us, she was concerned about Mr. Cole.

By dinner, the entire camp was upset about what had happened to Mr. Cole. When Capi explained it to the Singhs, Mrs. Singh went into another one of her blubbering fits. Wringing hands, running into the woods, sobbing about the dangers of guns and Africa. Mr. Singh chased after her, crying for her to be careful of wild animals. Mr. Norris complained about how he would regret this trip for the rest of his life. He and Austin retired early to their tents. No one knew where Baako was.

Capi, Jama and I settled down to a quiet meal.

When we finished, Capi asked me, "So, your father left you and your mother when you were a boy?"

I took a bite of wild game followed by a gulp of Guinness beer. I recounted my entire life from birth to the death of my mother. How I worshipped my father and the times we spent together. Then I told them about the day my father left. That brought tears to Jama's eyes. I stopped, tried to paste a recovery smile on my face. Something occurred to me. I eyed Capi with suspicion.

"Why do you want to know all this?"

"Well," she said, "I was curious about your father's life before he came here. You see," she said, pouring more wine, "I knew a different J.A. Quill than you described."

I leaned across the table. "You knew my father?"

My reaction didn't seem to surprise her.

"Not really well. I think I met him once, but only briefly. Cole and my husband knew him. Your father came to Kenya in 1946. They met him at an ivory auction."

The memory of the Mombasa train station and the mountains of ivory darkened my mood. "Was Cole and your husband poaching ivory with my father?"

She continued. "No. The selling of ivory wasn't illegal in those days, at least when it was sanctioned by the government. The Kenyan government was exporting hundreds of thousands of pounds of ivory. But the authorities controlled the harvesting through licensing. Whatever harvesting my husband and Cole did with your father was with government approval."

"So, your husband and Mr. Cole were in the ivory business with my father."

Capi took a deep breath. I looked at Jama. She buried her face in her hand.

Capi continued. "Yes. But, at first, they only sold pickup ivory."

"What's pickup ivory?"

"Ivory from elephants that died of natural causes."

Capi left her chair, nervously pacing in a circle, obviously not comfortable with the memories.

"Problem was," she said, "there wasn't enough pickup ivory to sustain a business. That's when your father started coming up with secret loads of ivory in numbers Cole and my husband had never seen before. Ivory that was not government sanctioned. When they asked where he got it, he made up stories that were obvious lies. This was when the government started cracking down on illegal poaching inside the newly established national parks. That's when my husband cut all business ties with J.A."

"Why didn't your husband turn my father into the authorities?" I said.

"When J.A. threatened Horace, he backed off."

I shook my head. "It's hard to believe my father would be involved in the killing of animals for money."

Capi gave me a twisted smile. "I'm sorry to tell you, he's the most notorious poacher in the history of East Africa. And the most ruthless."

A headache was coming on. The sort of headache that happens when a person's worst fears are realized.

"What about Mr. Cole?" I asked. "Did he end his relationship with my father?"

"Not exactly. Horace later found out Cole secretly continued to work with J.A. That's when my husband joined the Kenyan Wildlife Service as an assistant warden in charge of illegal poaching activities. A year later, he was..."

Capi stopped. She bent over, took a deep breath. Jama came to her side. Placed a hand on her shoulder. Capi took her daughter's hand, smiled at her.

"I'm okay, honey."

Capi continued.

"Horace was killed in a poaching raid in the Aberdare National Park." She swallowed hard. "He was alone when he came upon the poachers slaughtering a bull elephant. They..." She stopped, took a deep breath. "They hacked him to death with machetes. Two of the poachers responsible for killing him were caught by authorities. They claimed they were working for J.A Quill. He had given them orders to kill anyone who interfered with his business. Those men were scheduled to testify in court against your father but when the day of the trial came, they were found hanging in their jail cells. After that, Cole tried to distance himself from your father. But word was, J.A. still had his hooks in Cole."

Capi paused. Jama brought a glass of water for her mother. Capi drank it, then stared into the empty glass as if looking for some hidden answers there.

She continued.

"After my husband was killed, I was determined to see J.A. Quill brought to justice. Not just for poaching but for..." She shot me a sideways look. "There's no doubt in my mind that your father is responsible for my husband's death."

My headache got worse. I changed the subject.

"Back home," I said, "I worked in a zoo. There's this elephant I got very close to. Working with her, I came to understand how elephants think. Believe me, they're more human than some humans I've known. And the idea of someone killing her, cutting off her tusks just to make a buck is nothing less than barbaric."

Jama said, "So that's how you knew to handle the elephant that charged us."

Capi frowned. "What elephant?"

Jama realized her mistake. "Oh, Mother, I'm sorry. I was afraid to tell you at the time because I thought you'd be angry with Jack. But he was amazing. When you and the others were at the waterfall, an elephant came charging through the bush at us. I grabbed a rifle, but Jack stopped me from shooting it. He took charge. He started talking to the elephant, calmed it down. It seemed to understand him." She paused and smiled at me. "It was the strangest thing. Like their minds were as one."

I thought Capi would explode, but she didn't. She looked at Jama and said, "Okay. Well, thanks for telling me." Then she eyed me with renewed respect. "And thank you, Jack, for saving my daughter."

A moment of silence. We all had a lot to think about.

"So, what now?" I asked.

"Tomorrow morning, we leave early for Nairobi. We have to find your father soon and we don't have much time."

"Why the hurry?"

"We got a tip J.A. is about to meet this woman from China for an ivory sale. We need to find him as soon as possible to stop it. This woman buys millions of pounds of illegal ivory a year from poachers like your father. They call her the Ivory Lady. Word is he's about to sell her tons of illicit ivory and then he's going to disappear with his fortune."

"What can I do to help?"

Capi stood. "I don't know."

She glanced at the full moon. It had just cleared the treetops. "It's getting late. We should turn in. We'll get an early start in the morning."

When I got to my tent, I tried to sleep. Kept tossing and turning. I finally dozed only to be awakened by something hitting my tent. Like pebbles hitting the roof. I peered out through the flap. Jama stood outside. She whispered, "You want to take a walk?"

"Is it safe?"

"This from a man who stared an elephant down?"

I was out of the tent in record time.

We found a trail that led through a stand of trees out into a clearing. The horizon stretched as far as we could see. The sun had just died, leaving a blood-red sky. Acacia trees dotted the landscape. In the distance, the silhouettes of elephants, lions, giraffe moving through the darkness. The combination of sounds like night music. I knew those sounds would stay with me forever.

We stopped to enjoy the view.

"So beautiful," Jama said. "The magic of African nights." She closed her eyes, took a deep breath. "I've been to a lot of countries, but there's nothing to compare with an African sunset."

She faced me. "Is America as beautiful as Africa?"

"Yeah, but in a different way."

"How?"

"There's something ancient about this place. It seems sort of timeless."

"Yes. There is something primeval about it."

"That's a big word."

"It's true. Have you ever heard of Lucy of Ethiopia?"

"No. Is she a friend of yours?"

Jama laughed. "She's three million years old, silly."

"So, she's an old friend of yours."

She punched my shoulder. "No, crazy. She lived long ago in Africa. Her remains are considered evidence of one of the oldest human beings ever discovered. It makes you wonder. Did she enjoy the same sunsets we're looking at right now?"

"I wonder if she had a boyfriend whose mother kept hitting him?"

She pushed me this time. "You're impossible," she said.

She took my hand, pulled me close, laid her head on my shoulder. Not far away, a lion roared.

"We shouldn't stay out here too long," I said.

Without warning, she kissed me. I didn't resist.

"What was that for?" I asked.

"For saving my life."

On impulse, I kissed her.

"What was that for?" she said, laughing.

"For letting me."

We kissed several more times before starting back. We hadn't gone far when we passed a row of bushes. A rustling sound startled us.

"Did you hear that?" I said.

"Probably a bird."

As we hurried toward the campground, I glanced over my shoulder. I swear I saw Baako standing in the shadows, a long knife in one hand, the body of a snake in the other.

30.

MIDNIGHT. MY TENT. SLEEP came the minute my head hit the pillow. I dreamed. A desert island on a wide beach. Coconut trees. A man riding an elephant approached from a distance. He wore animal skins. He had an animal skin umbrella. My father. I ran toward him. When I got close, he slid off the elephant. Before I knew it, he grabbed one of the elephant's tusks, pulled on it. It separated from the animal and became a sword. My father plunged the ivory blade into my chest. He and the elephant laughed.

Something woke me. There are a lot of different sounds in the African nights. Most of them are easy to identify. Some belong to the human species. I thought it might be Jama again. Another nighttime walk? I could never get enough of her.

I got up, pulled on my pants, shirt, and shoes. Looked out of the tent. No one. Odd. I know I heard footsteps, human not animal. I got cautious real quick. Eased out of the tent looking both ways. I heard a sound but turned too late to see what was coming. Something hard hit my head and lights out.

I was moving. The sensation of traveling fast. A car motor, wheels hitting bumps. I opened my eyes. My head throbbed. I focused. Pain shot through my arms to my hands. My hands were tied behind me. Could it be Capi? Did she discover something new that turned her against me again? Damned, I couldn't win with that woman.

A man's voice. Heavy, husky.

"Boy, you okay?"

Another man with slurred speech. "I think he just woke up."

I turned my head. Two white guys were seated up front. The one in the passenger seat draining brown liquid from a bottle. Probably whiskey. I noticed a green blur moving fast. Trees. Lots of trees. Couldn't see much else.

"Where'd he say to drop him?"

These guys sounded American.

"Someplace remote on the savanna."

"Why there?"

"He wants him out of the way until his deal is done."

I passed out.

When I woke again, we were traveling over more bumpy roads. Finally, the truck stopped. Sunlight. The sun barely cleared the horizon. Someone grabbed me, picked me up. My first clear view of the men who had kidnapped me.

The tall one had a heavy beard. The other one, the drunk with eyes too close together, untied my hands. He pulled me out of the truck. I got my footing. I was standing by a beat-up army jeep. Around me, nothing but flat land, brown grass, a tree here and there.

I turned to the bearded one just in time to receive a big ham fist in my face. Knocked me down.

"What the hell?" I said.

He picked me up, grabbed my collar.

"Okay, kid, we got some questions to ask you and then we'll be on our way."

"Why did you hit me?"

"To get your attention."

I nursed my jaw. "Okay, I'm awake. Now, who the hell are you?"

The bearded one said, "We'll ask the questions."

The drunken guy said, "I don't think he knows who we are."

The bearded one said, "Of course he doesn't, idiot." He turned to me. "Do you know who we are?"

I shook my head. "No, I don't know who you are, idiot?"

He hit me again. I staggered, my hand over my eye. "Do you know who I am? I mean, maybe you got the wrong guy."

"Yeah, we know who you are," Beard said.

"I still don't know who you are," I said.

The drunk one held out his hand. "I'm Ernest. This is my brother, Robin."

Robin snapped at Ernest. "We're not supposed to use our names, dumbass. And you know not to call me that name."

"I forgot," Ernest said. He cupped his hand, and fake whispered to me, shooting a glance at his brother. "He thinks Robin's a girl's name."

I fake whispered. "So do I."

Robin hit me a third time. I fell to the ground, hard. He stood over me, finger pointing. "Don't ever call me that name again."

I felt my already aching jaw. Nothing seemed broken.

"I haven't called you anything yet," I said.

Robin ordered me to get up. I struggled to my feet.

"Sorry I hit you," Robin said, giving me a hand. "I'm just a little bit sensitive about my name. But you can call me Rob."

I said, "Rob, Robin, I don't give a shit what your name is. I just wanna know what the hell this is all about."

Rob-Robin faced Ernest. "Now that he knows our names, you know what we have to do."

"Yeah," Ernest said. "We have to kill him."

Rob-Robin shook his head. "No, dimwit. J.A said not to hurt him."

"Then what do we do with him?

"Just what J.A. said."

I asked them, "Are you talking about J.A. Quill?"

Rob-Robin said, "Uh-huh."

"That's my father," I told them.

"Yeah. We know. We work for him," Ernest said.

I was still groggy from being hit. I focused.

"What kind of work do you do for him?"

Rob-Robin said, "Kidnapping, murder. Stuff like that."

"Don't forget taking out the trash," Ernest said. "And walking the dog." He smirked at me. "Your father makes us to all his shit work."

"Shut up," Rob-Robin said. He said to me, "Your father wants some information from you and we don't have a lot of time."

"What information?"

"Do you know Phillip Cole?"

"Yeah."

"He used to work for your father."

"So?"

"You know Capi Lewis?" Rob-Robin asked.

"Uh-huh."

"So, you were there when Mason shot Cole. Right?"

"Yeah."

Rob-Robin shifted his weight. "Okay. So, we need to know what Cole said to Mrs. Lewis before he died."

"Cole's dead?"

Ernest said, "Yeah. Mason shot him."

"I know that," I said. "Why did Mason shoot Cole?"

Ernest said, "It weren't no accident."

Rob-Robin barked at his brother. "Shut up."

Ernest dropped his head, cowed. "Sorry."

Rob-Robin looked at me. "We need to know what Cole told Capi before he died?"

"Why?" I said.

"I told you," Rob-Robin said, "we'll ask the questions."

"I don't know what he told her," I said.

He slapped me. I reeled, caught my balance.

"You're lying?" he said.

"Jesus, I wish people would stop hitting me."

Ernest said, "We wanna know if Cole told Mrs. Lewis where J.A's compound is located."

Rob-Robin shouted at Ernest. "I just asked him that."

Ernest answered in a whiny voice. "No, you didn't."

Rob-Robin told me, "Mason said after he shot Cole, he was put in the back of his jeep. Then you and Capi Lewis hovered over Cole and he whispered something, but Mason couldn't hear it. What did Cole tell her?"

I said, "I don't know. I didn't hover. Capi hovered."

Rob-Robin said, "So, Capi hovered, but you didn't hover?"

"Right."

"Why didn't you hover?"

"Because Capi was hovering. There was no need for two hoverers," I said.

Ernest said, "He has a point."

Rob-Robin ignored him. He continued, "But if you didn't hover, then you couldn't have known what Cole said to Capi when she was hovering?"

My head was pounding. "That's what I told you. And enough with the hovering."

Rob-Robin took a moment to think. He seemed to have difficulty thinking. Finally, he asked, "Okay, if you didn't hear what Cole told Capi, and I don't know if I believe you, did Capi at least tell you what Cole told her?"

"Yes," I said, trying to sound irritated which I was.

"What was it?"

"Cole told Capi I was J.A. Quill's son."

"She didn't know that?"

"No," I said. "I stopped telling people who I was when I got here."

"When you got where?" Ernest asked.

"Africa," I said.

"Why didn't you tell people who you were?"

Fatigue was setting in. "It's a long story," I said.

Ernest said, "Are you ashamed of who you are?"

I said, "Frankly, yes."

Ernest looked at his brother. "Well, I don't want to be the one to tell J.A. his son is ashamed of him." He faced me. "You guys need to work that shit out."

Rob-Robin said to Ernest, "What are you, a family counselor?"

"I could've been," Ernest said in a whiny way.

Rob-Robin, arms folded, turned to his brother and said in the nicest way, "Could you possibly not say another word for the rest of our lives?"

Ernest took it hard. He bowed his head and stopped talking, at least for the moment.

Rob-Robin said to me, "Mason said Cole told him, before he died, you knew where your father's compound is."

"Cole lied."

Rob-Robin's mouth dropped. He got morbidly serious. "Men facing death don't lie."

"You're not about to quote Shakespeare, are you?"

"Who?"

"Never mind," I said. "Look, I swear on my mother's grave I don't know where my father's compound is. I didn't even know he had a compound. Ever since I got to Africa, people have asked me where my father is. I'm getting tired of it because if I knew where he was, I'd go there and beat the crap out of him for being a shitty father."

Rob-Robin stared at me. Ernest started to say something but thought better of it. But it was finally Ernest who broke the silence.

"I wish J.A. was my father," Ernst said.

"Well, you can have him," I said.

Ernest blurted out an explanation before his brother could stop him. His words were angry. "You should be a good son and tell us if you or someone you know knows where he is cause your father's about to close a big deal with this Chinese lady and if you or anyone else was to know where he is and tells the police…"

Rob-Robin jumped on Ernest, slapped his hand over his brother's mouth. "SHUT THE HELL UP!" he shouted.

Ernest got shifty-eyed, looking ashamed. Rob-Robin slowly removed his hand. Ernest grinned helplessly. Rob-Robin, hands on his hips, bent over, spit in the dirt. Took a moment, then focused on me.

"All right. I think you're probably telling the truth."

Ernest said, "Your father said you were an honest boy."

I said, "So, now that you believe me will you take me back to Nairobi?"

Rob-Robin shook his head. "No. That's not the plan."

"What plan?" I asked.

Rob-Robin said, "Your father knows why you came to Africa. And he wants you out of the way until he can finish with his deal and disappear."

"Why does he think I came to Africa?" I said.

Rob-Robin kicked dirt. "To kill him."

I shook my head. "I didn't come to kill him."

Ernest said, "Maybe you came to hurt him. You said you'd like to beat the crap out of him."

I felt ashamed. "I didn't mean that. I said it in anger."

Rob-Robin took up the thought. "So, what did you plan to do to him?"

"I'm not gonna discuss that with you."

"Why?" Rob-Robin said.

"Because it's personal."

Rob-Robin said, "Well, he told us to leave you here. By the time you get to Nairobi, J.A. will be gone." Rob-Robin turned to Ernest. "We're done."

They got in their jeep.

Rob-Robin said to his brother, "Give him the gun?"

Ernest got out of the truck and came back with a big rifle and a belt full of huge bullets. He shoved the rifle into my arms, slung the bullets over my shoulder.

"Be careful with that gun," he said. "It's got a helluva kick. Your father wanted you to have enough protection, so he gave you one of his prized possessions. That's an old but powerful .500 H&H. It'll kill an elephant."

"What's the H&H stand for?" I asked.

Ernest shrugged. "I don't know. His and hers?"

Rob-Robin said, "No, dumbass. It stands for Holland & Holland."

Ernest said, "Oh."

I told them, "You know, I can't believe my father would hire such dumb shits as you."

Ernest gave his brother a big grin. "That's what J.A. said. Only he called us dumbasses." He got serious, turned to me. "But he was just kidding."

I shook my head. "No, he wasn't."

Rob-Robin started the jeep.

I grabbed the door on the driver's side and said, "You're really gonna leave me here?"

"Somebody'll find you," Rob-Robin said. "It's Maasai country. They're everywhere."

I looked around. No caves, no bushes, vast empty land as far as I could see except for a landscape dotted with acacia trees.

"What if I need to start a fire or something?"

"Rub some sticks together," Rob-Robin said.

He gunned the truck, spun it around and headed the way they came.

I shouted, "Tell my father I still wanna see him."

They gave me the finger.

31.

SPREAD OUT BEFORE ME, the vast Kenyan savanna. Still early morning. I walked along the road for a while until I saw a lion in the distance. I don't know if it saw me, but I was taking no chances.

I spotted a lone acacia tree not far away. Lots of limbs. I hurried toward it. The limbs were higher than they appeared from a distance. I sat under the tree to rest. Clear skies, an easy wind, no beasts in sight.

I felt my pockets. No food. There was no water nearby. How long could I keep alive out here until someone finds me? The road wasn't exactly well traveled.

After the beatings I had taken the last few days, I was exhausted. I leaned against the tree and dozed off. Not sure how long I slept. Thought I had another dream, this time of thunder. The earth shook. I opened my eyes. I woke to the loudest thunder I'd ever heard. But it wasn't thunder. A massive herd of wildebeest headed straight for me. Thousands of them. The sound of their grunts like cows with sinus problems.

I moved fast. The limbs of the acacia tree didn't seem too high after all. I barely made it to the lower limb just as the mass of brown bodies galloped past me kicking up clouds of dust. I pulled my shirt over my head and waited it out.

It took a while for the herd to pass. I slipped down the tree trunk, checked for predators. All clear.

I started walking. Headed for a distant cluster of trees. It was so hot I had to make a lot of stops. Finally, I reached a line of trees along the banks of a river. The river water at this point ran swift. Not many animals lounging around in these rapids. The area seemed safe enough. I was thirsty, so it meant taking a chance on river water. What could go wrong?

I bent down at the river's edge. Cupped my hand and scooped up a drink of water. When I stood, a pair of eyes were looking at me. The scaly back of a crocodile emerged from a calm pool on the opposite bank. I wasn't thirsty after all.

I was worn out. A nearby acacia tree proved the best spot to rest. The heavy gun had become a burden. I examined it. A gift from dear 'ol Dad. How sweet. If I hadn't thought it was needed I would've thrown it in the river. But I knew there were lions around, so I removed two of the cigar-size bullets from the belt, opened it and filled the two barrels with ammo, snapped it shut, found the safety. I pulled on the safety button hoping it was off. I leaned up against the tree with the big gun on my lap. It felt kinda good. Powerful, safe feeling. I was ready for anything. Lions, leopards, buffalo.

I fell asleep.

I woke up to the distant brassy sound of an elephant. For a moment, it felt like I was in Virginia at the zoo and Betty was calling.

My eyes were half open. I blinked. Cleared my vision. Buzzards circling. A few drifting clouds. A slight wind pushed through the trees. About thirty yards away, a lion.

He was staring at me, hunched over in a stalking crouch. I tried to stand. My knees were rubber. Where's the rifle? In my lap. The bullet belt slung over my shoulder. The lion, on his belly, inched closer. His eyes riveted on me. I thought of the lions back in the zoo. They loved me. That's because I fed them. This lion? He loves me too because I'm about to feed him. Me.

I kept my eyes on him as I fumbled for the rifle. The safety. Was it on or off? I gathered the strength in my legs. Pushed up using the tree trunk. The lion stood. Probably waiting for me to run. I kept saying to myself, whatever you do, don't run. Whatever you do, don't run. Whatever you do...

I ran.

I ran like hell. Heard the lion coming after me. Knew it was only seconds before he had me in his jaws. I took a chance, a big chance. I stopped, turned, shouldered the gun. The lion was about to go airborne. I pulled the trigger. An enormous explosion. The recoil of the big gun catapulted me backward. For one unforgettable moment, I was airborne. I remember my head hitting something solid. Then the world went dark.

32.

I WOKE UP ON my back to morning light. The sound of birds chirping. Clouds, beautiful clouds pushed by a cool breeze. I was breathing, alive. Or was it heaven? Or something like it? I pushed up on an elbow. Scanned the area. Nothing.

More buzzards circling. I wondered if an animal had died. Caught something out of the corner of my eye.

The lion.

Oh, hell, I thought. The lion lying on its stomach only a few feet away staring at me with bloodlust in its eyes. Was it about to spring? My gun. Where was my gun? I tried to find it. It was at my feet between me and the lion. I didn't move. Maybe he thought I was dead. But why would he wait all night without making me his dinner? Or breakfast? It made no sense. I took another look at the beast. Glassy, lifeless, chilling eyes. Something strange about this lion. Like he was...

Dead?

I got to my feet. Tiptoed toward him as if tiptoeing would not wake him if he were alive. I carefully examined him. He was dead alright.

A big sigh of relief. I buried my face in my hands. Then I realized I had just killed an innocent animal. All he wanted was breakfast. Even though I had denied him that, I'm glad I did. But still…

I bent over him. Touched him. He was cold. I felt bad. This magnificent animal taken before his time. I heard hissing sounds. Looked up. A flock of vultures perched nearby on an acacia tree waiting for lunch. There was nothing I could do for the lion. I bent on one knee, patted it on the head and told it, "Sorry, fella, it was me or you."

A noise. Footsteps. I turned around.

"Shit."

Standing nearby, calm, silent. Baako.

"Where the hell did you come from? You scared the crap out of me."

Baako said, "So did the lion."

I looked at my pants. "Oh."

Baako turned and walked away at a fast pace. I assume he wanted me to follow him. I shouldered my rifle and ammo belt and ran after him.

Baako was walking at a normal pace. I had to run to keep up. At almost seven feet tall, his stride was twice that of mine. I was like a puppy trying to catch the big dog.

The savanna stretched for miles in front of us. It must have been noon. The grass was getting hot.

"Where are we headed?" I asked.

"My village."

"How much farther?"

"Not far."

Baako continued. He headed toward a point on the distant horizon. In his right hand, a spear. Slung over my shoulder, the heavy gun. Over the other shoulder, the gun belt. They seemed heavier than usual. I thought of dumping them. Sweat poured down my face. My legs finally gave out. I collapsed in a cloud of dust.

Baako stopped and watched me with no emotion.

"Can't go on," I mumbled. "Give me a minute."

He waited. I struggled to stand. Then almost fell again.

"Sorry," I said. "Not used to this."

Baako turned and resumed his trek. I fell into line. It wasn't long before I had to stop again. My lungs were close to bursting. Baako finally stopped and waited for me. My head throbbed. I dropped my rifle. Removed my bullet belt, threw it on the rifle. Fell on my ass.

Baako picked up the rifle and bullets. "You will need this."

He continued on. I stumbled to my feet. Without the gun and bullets, I was able to catch up to him.

"Where did you learn English?" I asked, almost out of breath.

"From the English."

"All this time I didn't know you could talk."

"You talk too much."

We walked for more than an hour before reaching Baako's village. It was visible from half a mile away. The village was surrounded by a web of thorn bushes. We headed for an opening.

Inside, a circle of huts covered in sticks, mud and what appeared to be animal skins. Women, some in bright clothing, others drab brown skins, busy carrying baskets, working on the huts, doing various chores. When Baako and I entered, a small band of men holding spears surrounded us. They chattered wildly, raising and lowering their spears. They calmed down when Baako raised his hand. He spoke to them for a long time. What he said, I don't know, but some of the men didn't seem to agree with him.

"What did you say to them?" I asked.

"How you killed a lion with your rifle. You are lucky the lion didn't eat you."

"Sorry to disappoint them."

A very tall man in the group stepped forward. His hair hung in finely wound ropes. He was much older than the others. Carried a spear with a large iron tip and wooden shaft. Wagged his finger in Baako's face, his words angry. Baako listened until the man backed off, giving me a savage look. I met the man's stare head-on, but I was trembling inside.

I said to Baako, only my lips moving, "What's with this guy?"

Baako said, "He said a big gun not makes you a man. Real man kills with a spear, not with gun."

"I guess I'm not a real man then," I said.

"He knows this," Baako said.

The man raised his spear, shaking it. He grunted something.

Baako said to me, "Now we teach you how to be a man."

"What does that mean?"

The spear carrier made a kind of yelping sound. A group of women appeared. They grabbed me, pulling me away from the men. I looked at Baako, pleading. "Where are they taking me?"

They dragged me into a large mud tent. At least I thought it was mud until I stepped inside. The smell almost knocked me over.

Against my will, the women took my clothes off. They giggled during the process. I didn't. Out came the Maasai clothes. A bright red robe wrapped around my lower body. Sandals and some beads. They tied a band around my head then forced me out of the hut. They pushed me toward the group of warriors.

Baako stood emotionless, holding his spear. When the women retreated, the warriors formed a circle. Two of the younger men entered the circle and began to jump. When one jumped high, the other jumped higher. They sang as they jumped. At one point, Baako pushed me into the circle. A young Maasai warrior joined me. He jumped very high, about three feet. At close to six and a half feet tall, he bounced in the air so high I thought he might injure himself coming down. Baako motioned for me to jump. My first attempt proved feeble. The laughter stung. I tried again. Better. Again, getting the hang of it. I eventually almost matched my opponent's altitude. The old warrior raised his spear. The jumping stopped.

Baako said to me, "Now we teach you how to kill a lion the Massai way. Without a gun."

If you've never thrown a spear, it's not easy. Baako led me to a large tree with a wide trunk. It was called a baobab tree. The young group of warriors were already lined up for target practice. The head warrior pointed to me. He wanted me to go first. Baako handed me a spear. I must have grabbed it the wrong way. Baako showed me how to clutch the thing, then how to throw it.

The baobab tree was about ten yards away. Baako took his spear, threw it at the tree, plunging it dead into the trunk. He nodded to me. My turn. I gripped the wooden part of the spear as he showed me, wound up as if throwing a baseball, and let it fly. It not only fell short, it missed the tree by a good five feet.

Another round of laughter from the peanut gallery.

Baako made a gesture with his spear for me to try again. I ran out and retrieved my spear. This time I used a football throw. I was on the goal line, throwing a bomb to my receiver about a hundred yards out. The spear flew wildly, hitting the trunk of the tree sideways, skittering off to the right. Again, with the laughter. I was their afternoon entertainment.

Baako joined his fellow warriors. I followed just in time to get out of the way. The tribe launched a volley of spears. Each drove into the trunk with such precision all landed within a foot-wide circle.

Baako looked at me. "Now we hunt a lion."

I hesitated. "Okay, as long as we don't have to hurt it."

His tribal friends could really run. I mean fast. I had no choice but to follow. We headed toward an open savanna. By the time they stopped, my lungs were about to give out.

They stared for a long time at a field of knee-high grass. Without warning, the tribe began to chant, shaking their spears as they moved forward through the grass toward some unseen form. Half of them broke away, headed to the right and around the object of their focus. A loud roar. The object rose from the bush. A lion, a big lion. It must have been asleep. The warriors surprised the animal before it could react. Too late, the animal was surrounded.

The warriors encircled the confused, angry lion. It was a large male. It wheeled in a circle, growling, lunging, backing away from the chorus of spears jabbing at it. Baako joined the line, thrusting his weapon to within inches of the lion's body. The circle closed.

I stood away from the action. Baako motioned me forward. I shook my head. I wanted no part of killing this magnificent creature or of it killing me. Too late. The circle opened. The lion, seeing a way out, focused on you-know-who. I either had to run or become his lunch. It started toward me. As it did, the circle of warriors opened up, grew larger, then eventually enclosed me in the ring with the lion. The chants increased to a fever pitch, spears stabbing at the enraged beast. I looked at Baako. He made a thrusting motion with his spear, urging me to join in the attack. I went rigid. Fear gripped me. I shook so hard my spear slipped out of my hand. The lion zeroed in on me. I wondered what it would be like to be eaten alive. Would he start with my legs? I would. Or maybe go for the throat? Thankfully, I would never know. The circle broke, the lion saw his escape, took it and disappeared into the brush.

I fell to my knees, overcome with relief. The warriors gathered around me. I remained frozen to the spot, unable to release the tension in my muscles. I finally regained control of my body and voice. My words were a jumble of fear and confusion.

"What was... What? I... Did I? The lion... Was he...?"

"The lion is gone," Baako said.

I managed a deep breath. Calmed my nerves, slowed my racing heart.

I said to Baako, "Why did you let him go?"

"No need to kill the lion."

"But you said I needed to kill a lion without a gun to become a man."

"You are already a man."

"Then what was this all about?"

"Just messing with you, Jack."

The warriors grinned.

33.

WHEN WE GOT TO the village, a group of women ushered me into a hut. On the ground, my clothes. After they left, I dressed in my pants, shirt, and boots. My rifle and bullets were missing.

I left the hut to find Baako. He was standing outside, holding my rifle and ammo belt.

"You will need these," he said.

I slung the rifle over my shoulder, the belt across my chest. I noticed a group of warriors assembled, looking fierce in headdresses and beads carrying spears, bows and arrows, knives. Baako had a new spear. Longer and more deadly looking.

"What's going on?" I asked.

"You follow."

Without another word, the warriors, led by Baako, took off running through the opening in the thorn barrier. I had no choice. I followed.

Trying to keep up with this crowd proved almost impossible. They were Olympic class sprinters. Daylight had almost played out. We were headed north into darkness. By the time we stopped, we had left the savanna, entering an area of lush forest and rolling hills. I'm not sure how far we travelled, but it had to be at least several miles. The full moon gave off enough light to see. Baako and company came to rest among a thicket full of bushes.

They huddled together, silent, listening. Not far away, the faint sounds of humans moving among the trees. When they passed, I whispered to Baako.

"Who are they?"

"Shiftas."

"What are Shiftas?"

"Poachers," he said.

We made camp not far away. Baako barked at one of the young warriors. The man disappeared into the woods. Returned with sticks in one hand, dark lumps in another. He dropped the lumps on the ground and rubbed the sticks together. It took a while, but eventually the wood mixed with the lumps began to burn. It didn't smell that bad. I asked Baako what it was.

"Elephant dung."

He dug into a bag for something. Brought out a chunk of meat. Pulled a knife, cut a slice of the meat and gave it to me. I wanted to ask what it was but thought better of it. The others settled around the fire, also taking food from bags. We ate in silence. The meat was tasty enough, but it was greasy with fat. When the warriors were done, they slept in a circle on the ground. I found a spot near the fire and fell asleep.

Dawn. Someone kicked my leg. It was Baako. They were waiting for me. I rolled over. A circle of giants stared at me.

"We must go," Baako said.

Without another word, they ran away. I jumped up, found my rifle and ammo belt, and did my best to catch up.

More running. Hours of it. We were in wooded, hilly territory. When the hills became almost vertical, the warriors slowed down but not much. I struggled to keep up. I almost lost sight of them.

They stopped around noon to eat. I came plodding into their circle. I sat. Baako drank from a bag made of skin. He offered me some. I thought it was water. Turned out it was blood mixed with cow's milk. It wasn't half bad.

Continuing the run. Another two hours of painstaking movement through bushes, a stand of trees, across stretches of open country. A moment for rest.

I asked Baako, "Where are we going?"

"You will see."

Two more hours of running and walking. In the distance, gunfire. The distinct screams of elephants. We hurried forward.

Finally, Baako stopped, held up his hand. We gathered around him. We stood like statues among a stand of eucalyptus trees waiting for his command. The sound of machines, gunfire was close. Men shouting. More screams of elephants, sounding like cries of pain. Baako motioned for us to move forward. We reached the edge of a steep hill. Below us, a clearing ringed by trees. The scene in the valley was a horror show.

Scattered throughout the clearing were the mutilated bodies of several elephants. There must have been a dozen fallen elephants, some barely alive. Africans armed with machetes and handsaws chopped at the feet of the dead ones. Several used saws grinding away at the huge tusks. Butchers with rifles moved among the bodies firing pointblank into the heads of the elephants still alive. Supervising the slaughter, a white man dressed in safari gear. Pith helmet, khaki shorts, hunting jacket, smoking a pipe. Strapped to his side, a pistol. He ambled around the clearing, inspecting the work of the killers as if taking an afternoon walk in the park. An elephant cow stood to the side watching her mate being carved up. She rocked back and forth, huffing, grunting, raising her trunk in protest. The white man grabbed a rifle from a worker. He walked up to the distressed female and shot her between the eyes. She slumped over almost on top of a baby elephant. It ran out of the way only to return to its mother, trying in vain to wake her. The white man loaded another round into the rifle chamber and shot the baby. It fell at the feet of its mother.

I dropped to my knees, overcome at the horror of these magnificent animals being destroyed.

"Jack."

I turned. Baako stood over me.

"Can you shoot?" he asked.

I took a deep breath and got to my feet. I took the .500 H&H off my shoulder. Quickly loaded both barrels with the deadly rounds. Looked Baako squarely in the eyes. I nodded.

The warriors stood in silence for a moment. Baako moved among them, speaking softly in their native language. Two of them carried bows and arrows. The others, spears.

Baako turned to me.

"You wait here."

"When do I shoot?"

Baako said, "You will know."

Before he left, he said, "Do not shoot the white man."

The warriors followed Baako around the rim of the valley. They started down the slope, then disappeared into the trees. I moved to the edge overlooking the carnage. I kneeled on the ground with a clear view of everything happening below. I checked my rifle to make sure the safety was off.

The attack by the warriors was swift. One moment a worker chopping at an elephant's tusk. A second later an arrow sliced through his throat. More of the workers fell to arrows, spears and knives. Baako's warriors spread out through the valley, attacking without mercy.

I searched for the white man. Couldn't locate him. Time for me to engage. I spotted a large native worker, rifle pointed at Baako. Baako didn't see him. I leveled the H&H double at him, braced myself for the recoil, and fired. I missed. But the blast from the gun caught his attention. He turned to see where it came from. He spotted me. Raised his rifle in my direction. It was too late. Baako had heard the loud report of the Holland. He saw the man pointing his gun at me. He threw his knife. It plunged into the man's right side, buried deep into his chest. The man turned to look at Baako as if upset at being interrupted. Then he fell dead.

While that played out, the white man appeared. He'd been hiding in the carved-out carcass of a bull elephant. He reared his head in time to see Baako signaling to me. The white man pulled a pistol, aimed at Baako. My second chance to save my friend.

I remembered Baako's order not to shoot the white man. I aimed a bit to the right of him, pulled the trigger on my second barrel. The bullet slammed into the dirt short of the dead elephant's carcass. The white man ducked for cover. Baako walked directly toward him. The man began to fire at Baako as he marched toward him. The white man emptied his pistol. All the shots missed.

Baako was on him. Grabbed the man, took his pistol, dragged him away from the elephant's body, threw him on his knees. The white man shook violently, staring up at this giant of a man who could not be killed by bullets.

By the time I reached the valley floor, the battle was over. None of the warriors suffered wounds. But the elephant killing crew were dead or had run away.

I walked among the dead, human and animal. The poachers suffered arrows and spears to the body, the neck and to the head. The elephants were far more disfigured. Heads hacked off. Tusks sawn away. Feet severed. Stacks of ivory ready to haul away. The sheer size and number of dead giants was staggering. So much blood pooled into small red ponds.

I noticed the warriors standing silently in a nearby clearing.

I heard crying.

I hurried to the spot where they surrounded the white man who was on his knees, his hands covering his face, sobbing. Baako stood over him, a knife in one hand, the man's pistol in the other.

"Please. Please don't kill me," the man begged.

Baako studied him. "I know this man. He was a safari hunter."

"Why would he turn to poaching?"

"Money."

Baako spoke to him in his native Maasai language. The man understood. He answered Baako.

I asked, "What did he say?"

The man appeared to notice me for the first time. His eyes widened.

"Oh, thank God. A white man," he said. "I tried to tell him I'm a member of The King's Rifles."

"I don't know what that is," I said.

The man gave me a second look. "You're not British."

"No," I said.

When the man spoke, his mouth made bubbles. His nose was running. On his knees, he was now the pathetic victim. He pleaded with me and Baako.

"Please. I know how this looks. But I was just doing my job."

I reached down and grabbed his shirt, pulling him to his feet.

"You call murdering innocent animals a job? That's not a job. That's a crime against nature."

He whimpered.

"Who do you work for?" I said.

"I don't know."

"You're lying. Who's your boss?"

He swallowed hard. "I really don't know. He's just a voice on a dog."

"On a what?" I asked.

"Oh. You're American. A dog is a telephone. He's just a voice on the telephone. I'm what you Yanks would call a middleman."

I released him. He fell to his knees.

"What's your name?" I asked.

He was breathing hard. Sat up and took off his helmet. He was sweating. Mopped his face with his sleeve.

"Percy Yates."

"So, Mr. Yates, you're just a middleman."

He nodded. "What are they going to do with me?"

"I don't know," I said. "What do they usually do with murderers in this country?"

"Murderer?" Yates frowned. "I'm not a murderer. These are animals."

I felt like kicking him.

"How many elephants have you killed?"

"We have people for that."

"You just supervise. Right?"

"Right." He nodded like his answer cleared him of guilt.

I bent over, looking him in the face. He looked away.

"I saw you shoot the female. And then you shot the baby. What sort of monster shoots a baby elephant?"

He shrugged, his body quivering. "I did it a favor. How long you think that baby would have survived without its mother?"

I couldn't help myself. I punched him in the face so hard he went flying into the dust. Baako's warriors picked him, shoving him to his knees. Yates studied the faces looking down on him. He knew he wasn't getting out of this in one piece.

"Look," he said, wiping blood away, "if you want the man behind all of this, I only have a name."

I gave him a wicked stare.

He said, "Have you ever heard of a man by the name of Quill?"

"Quill?" I said. "Do you mean J.A. Quill?"

Yates perked up.

"Yes. That's the man. He runs this whole operation."

"Where is this J.A. Quill?" I asked.

Yates shrugged. "I don't know. Nobody I know has ever seen him."

"You just take your orders from him."

He nodded. "Yeah. On the dog. I mean the telephone. But I don't know if it's him on the phone."

I wheeled around and stuck my face right up to his, gritting my teeth. "I think you know exactly where he is. And I'm gonna give you about two seconds to tell me or my friends here will get it out of you one way or the other."

Yate's mouth dropped. His eyes became saucers. The sweat poured down his face.

He pleaded, "I swear, if I knew, I'd tell you."

I threw up my hands. Looked at Baako. "Do what you want to him."

Baako makes a scissor motion with his index and middle finger. Yates went pale.

"What does that mean?" he asked, looking at me?

I shrugged. "A haircut?"

Yates lets out a pitiful sound and threw up. The warriors grabbed him, pulled him to his feet. Yates went berserk.

"No, no. Please. Don't do that." Yates is frantic. He pleaded with me. "You're a white man. Are you going to let these savages do this?"

I looked at Baako. Yate's pistol was still in Baako's hand. I grabbed it. Took Yates by the collar. Shoved he gun barrel under his chin. Cocked the hammer.

"Who did you say were savages?"

The man started to shake. "I... I'm sorry. I... I didn't mean to say that."

"Now," I said, "tell me where I can find J.A. Quill."

His voice trembled. "I swear, I don't know."

I pushed him away. He fell back on his knees. I uncocked the pistol and threw it on the ground. Nodded to Baako.

"He's all yours."

The warriors pulled the man's pants down. He started crying. He closed his eyes, stood half naked, trembling.

"Please," he begged. "I don't know where he is, but I have some information."

I held up my hand for Baako to stop. He backed off. Yates pulled up his pants. Dug into a pocket. Took out a small notebook. Gave it to me.

"What's this?"

"A tally book."

"What's a tally book?"

Yates breathed so hard his words came in spurts. "For... For keeping... records," he said.

I opened it. It was full of numbers.

"What kind of records?" I asked.

He swallowed hard, his face wrinkled in fear. He gagged, then dry retched.

Shaking the book in his face, I screamed at him. "What kind of records?"

"Numbers," he said.

I thumbed through the book.

"Jesus. These are lists of elephants you've killed. There are hundreds. How many?"

He bowed his head. "I don't know the exact number we've harvested."

"Harvested?" I shook my head. "This isn't wheat. They're living, breathing creatures."

I examined one page. It appeared to be calculations on how much ivory and the money each tusk was worth. There was a symbol I'd seen before. Not like a dollar sign. More like a fancy L with a slash through it. Again, I shoved the page in front of Yates' nose. I pointed to the symbol.

"What is this?"

His throat was dry, voice pinched.

"A pound sign. Like your American dollar."

"So, this represents money. Right?"

He nodded. "Uh-huh."

"How much money in American dollars?"

Yates moved his mouth like he was counting.

"I guess… Uh, about six. Maybe seven."

"Six or seven what?"

He didn't want to say it. He gave me a weak smile. His eyelids slowly closed. He was exhausted.

"Six or seven what?" I asked.

He shrugged. "Million."

"Dollars?"

He nodded, glancing at Baako. Baako stood, arms folded, glaring at Yates.

"Are you telling me this Quill fellow is worth millions of dollars from ivory?"

Yates nodded.

I hurried through the pages of the book, not wanting to believe the sordid details. I glared at Yates. "Good lord, man, what kind of monster are you?"

His eyes begged for mercy. "I was a very… respectable… big game hunter. Important clients. All legal. My own… safari company." The man could hardly breathe. He looked at Baako. His voice squeaked. Yates said something to Baako in Maasai Maa.

Yates turned to me. He tilted his head toward Baako. "I remember him. He worked for me. I was famous."

I turned to the last page. Another number. I pointed to it. "What's this?"

Yates squinted at the number. "Phone number."

"Whose number is it?"

"I don't know."

"Who answers?"

"A man. I don't know who it is."

"Could it be J.A. Quill?" I asked.

"Maybe." He pleaded. "Please. I'm only the..."

I interrupted. "The middleman."

I stuffed the tally book into my back pocket. I nodded to Baako. Baako signaled to his warriors. They pulled Yates' pants down again. He screamed, arms flapping like a wounded goose. He tried to push the warriors away. Baako, knife in hand, faced Yates. I turned away, not wanting to watch. A horrific scream followed by mournful sobbing. The screaming didn't stop until Baako was finished.

Footsteps behind me. I turned. Baako stood before me. Past him, I saw Yates on his knees, his pants still at his ankles, blood streaming down his leg. For a moment, I forgot he was a murderer. I felt a pang of sorrow for the poor guy. The shame for a man to lose that body part. Baako's right arm was at his side, holding the knife. He raised his left arm. In his hand, a jagged piece of gore dripping blood dangling between his fingers. As disgusting as it appeared, my curiosity kicked in. I squinted, focused. I wasn't sure what I was looking at. I moved closer to the gruesome thing.

"What the hell is that?" I asked Baako.

"Emorata."

"What?"

"Circumcision," Baako said.

I backed away, not believing what I heard.

"You circumcised him?" I did the scissor thing with my fingers. I said, "I thought you cut off his, you know, his thing?"

Baako frowned.

"No, Jack. We are not savages."

I laughed.

Baako didn't.

34.

THE WARRIORS TIED YATES and put him in the back of a jeep left by the poachers. Baako gave me directions to Nairobi. I said goodbye and took off. I came to a main road and stopped. I looked at Yates. His khaki shorts were blood-soaked.

"How long will it take to get to Nairobi?" I asked him.

He managed to raise his head. "Three maybe four hours."

I gunned the jeep and headed up the dusty road.

Not long into our trip, a rain shower. The dirt road turned into a mudslide. I slugged along, struggling through the rain. We hit a stretch of road covered with boulders and volcanic dust. On either side of the road, bushes, fields of rock, and towering trees that appeared to explode from the ground. Ahead, a long, straight road and nothing in sight. The next sixty miles were nothing more than dirt paths. When the rain stopped, I suffered through heat and the groaning and moaning of Yates who went from sleep to painful bouts of waking to his misery. I knew we were getting near civilization when we passed a man leading a cow on a rope. I pulled up alongside him. He was obviously Maasai.

"You speak English?" I said.

He stopped, stared.

I turned to Yates. He was asleep. I punched him awake. His eyes opened.

"Hey, ask this guy where we are."

Yates raised his head. "Where are we?"

"How the hell should I know?" I screamed. "But this guy probably knows."

Yates mumbled something to the guy in Maa. The man pointed ahead.

"So, how far to a town?" I asked.

Yates shook his head.

"Maasai don't know distances. Only directions."

I checked the gas gauge. "Damned. We're almost out of gas."

Yates groaned. Closed his eyes. The man with the cow walked on.

I hit the pedal and started down the road. I didn't get far. The jeep gurgled then died.

Once again, I turned to Yates.

Shouting, I said, "Wake up asshole. We're out of gas."

Yates opened one bloodshot eye. "You need to get to Narok," he said. "It's not far. Get gas there," he said. He closed his eye.

I sat for a while staring at a hot, empty sky and vacant land. The heat was getting to me. I jumped out and dragged Yates from the car. He came awake fast.

"What are you doing?" he said.

"We're going for gas."

"Are you crazy? Look at me. I'm in no shape to walk. I'll never get there."

"I'm gonna need you to translate for me when we get to town," I told him.

"Don't make me do this. I'll die."

"Then you'll die trying."

Yates' knees buckled. He groaned in pain. Out of frustration, I slapped him and then felt ashamed for doing it. I reached out a hand to help him up. He collapsed again, rolling into a ball of agony. I heard a sound. I turned to see the man with the cow. He had caught up to us. I figured he saw me mistreat Yates. I felt a pang of guilt.

I said to the man, "He's a bad man. I was just trying to…"

The man with the cow stared, no expression. The cow seemed more interested than his keeper. I pointed down the road.

"Narok?" I said to the man.

The man nodded.

As he passed by me, I said to him, "I don't normally treat people this way."

He continued walking, pulling the cow.

I grabbed Yates and yanked him to his feet. He yelped.

"Come on," I said, "let's go."

I took him by the sleeve and started after the man with the cow. A couple of hours later we staggered into the town of Narok.

Narok was a small village swarming with people. Dozens of children, men, women, goats, cows, sheep, dogs. Cow dung everywhere. Yates struggled to walk. He finally stopped.

"I can't go any farther," he said.

I grabbed him by the shoulders. "You've been here before, right?"

He nodded.

"Where can I find gas?"

Yates straightened. Looked around. He was breathing hard. Me too. The heat had reached my bones. Yates nodded toward a flat building with a flag hanging over the door.

"The guy in there. He'll know."

We both stumbled into a cramped room. There was nothing but a desk and a man asleep in a chair. A fly landed on his face. On the wall, an ancient-looking wall phone. I cleared my throat. The man woke up, glared at me.

I smiled and said, "Hello, sir. Is there a gas station around here?"

He sat up, rubbed his eyes. He nodded. Pointed ahead.

"Thank you," I said.

The gas station wasn't much of a station. It was more like a shed. There was a guy guarding a beat-up antique of a gas pump. Yates spoke to the man in Maasai. After a heated exchange, Yates paid the man and pointed to a can. He told me I would have to trek back to the jeep without him. Claimed he couldn't take another step. I didn't have the energy to argue. I picked up the can and started for the jeep. It must have weighed ten pounds. On the way, a safari party passed me carrying a group of tourists. They smiled and waved. They didn't bother stopping.

It wasn't long before I drove into Narok. When I stopped at the gas pump, no Yates. I asked the gas attendant where the white man was. He said the white man got a ride on a safari. Son-of-a-bitch. I needed more gas. I asked the man how much to fill the tank. He mentioned something about shillings. I didn't know what that meant. I searched my pockets. The tally book was still there with a few dollars. I handed a dollar to the gas man. He shook his head. I gave him two more. Again, he refused. I finally got him to agree to five dollars. I filled the tank and was about to get on the road when I thought of the tally book. Then the office and the flag. And the wall phone. I had an idea.

The man behind the desk was asleep again. I cleared my throat. This time he didn't wake up. I went to the wall phone and picked up the receiver. A woman's voice asked me what number I was calling. I got the tally book and found the phone number. I gave it to the woman and listened as the phone on the other end rang. Finally, a voice.

"Yeah?"

People forget a lot of things. Years wear away our memories. A lot of what we've heard or read or thought disappears into the fog of the past. But one thing you never forget. The voice of someone you love.

"Dad?"

Silence, then in a voice buzzing through a bad connection, "Who is this?"

"Dad, it's me. Jack."

Silence.

Here was my chance. The reason I came to Africa. To make my father pay for breaking my mother's heart. Only, it seemed lame to try to make him pay over a phone with a bad connection in the middle of nowhere. But it was probably going to be the only chance I had to let him know the grief he had caused my mother.

"Dad? You still there?"

I heard him clear his throat.

"I know it's you," I said. "Talk to me."

Nothing.

I actually dreaded telling him. But he needed to hear it.

"Dad. Mom's dead. She died waiting for you to come home."

Dead silence. I could hear him breathing. My eyes filled with tears.

"You broke her heart."

The phone sputtered. Static. A clicking sound. The phone went silent. It was like when he left me eleven years ago. The same sound of a door closing.

I hung up the phone.

The man asleep at the desk was snoring.

35.

IT WAS LATE AFTERNOON when I rolled into Nairobi. The city streets were jammed with automobiles. Crowds lined the sidewalks. The sound of a brass band, people shouting, screaming, applauding, their attention on a procession of fancy automobiles coming down the street. Turned out Princess Elizabeth was in town. People were lined up to get a glimpse of royalty.

I rerouted, found a back street. Stopped and asked a bystander direction to the Norfolk hotel. I hoped to locate Capi and Jama when I got there.

After winding through streets to avoid the crowds, I finally pulled the jeep to a stop in front of the Norfolk. I hurried into the lobby. Shirley was at the front desk.

"Hi, Shirley."

She looked surprised. She winked, leaned forward on the desk. In a low voice said, "Doctor Livingston, I presume?"

She laughed. I managed a weak smile. Then she noticed my appearance. She frowned.

"Oh, Mr. Sims, are you okay?"

"Yeah. By the way, have you seen Capi? I mean Mrs. Lewis."

Shirley nodded. "She's in Mr. Cole's office."

"Thanks," I said.

I started toward the hallway.

Shirley said, "It's really sad about Mr. Cole."

I stopped. "Yeah. Really sad," I said and headed for Cole's office.

I knocked on the door. Footsteps. The door opened. It was Capi.

"Jack." She grabbed me and pulled me in. "Where the hell have you been? We woke up in camp the other morning and you were gone."

Sitting in chairs in front of Mr. Cole's desk, Jama and two men in uniforms. Another man, a tall African dressed in military gear, stood behind them at attention.

Jama ran to me, gave me a big hug.

"Jack, I'm so glad you're okay," she said. She was near tears.

I held her close. "I'm alright," I said.

Jama pulled back, studying me. "You look awful, Jack."

I kissed her on the forehead.

"I feel awful," I said.

I noticed three men in the room. They wore uniforms. Two were seated. The other stood behind them at attention.

"Who are you?" I asked.

Jama said, "Oh, Jack, this is Warden Hastings, Ranger Ngari and behind them is Lieutenant Kendi."

The two seated men stood. The Warden was white, definitely British, moustache and all. The other, Ranger Ngari, an African. We shook hands. The Lieutenant remained at attention.

Warden Hastings and Ranger Ngari sat. Jama led me to a chair opposite them. We sat. She patted me on the shoulder. Capi took the chair behind Cole's desk across from us.

Capi said, "So, Jack? Are you going to tell us what happened?"

"Take your time," Jama said. Just the sound of her voice relaxed me. I took a deep breath.

"I was kidnapped," I told them.

"What?" Capi said.

As I told the story, Ngari took notes in a small notebook. Hastings stood, arms folded, listening intently. I explained how these two men who worked for my father came into camp the other night and knocked me out. They threw me in a jeep and took me to the Maasai Mara where they questioned me. They were trying to learn if I knew where my father was located. When I finally convinced them I didn't know, they abandoned me in the middle of nowhere with only a rifle and a belt full of bullets. Luckily, Baako found me.

Hastings asked, "Who is Baako?"

Capi said, "He was Cole's Maasai gunbearer." She leaned across the desk. "Jack. Cole is dead."

"Yeah, I know."

"How do you know?" she said.

"Those guys told me."

Hastings stood, started pacing. He stroked his moustache, obviously thinking. He stopped, looked at Capi.

"That confirms our suspicions. J.A. is getting ready to run."

"Run where?" I asked.

Capi spoke. "Who knows? Probably Europe, the Far East, somewhere he can't be found."

Warden Hastings said, "We believe he's meeting with a woman from the Far East who goes by the name Ivory Lady. He's about to sell her tons of ivory and when he does…"

I held up my hand. "Capi told me all about it."

Hastings threw me a disapproving glance. Military men don't like inferiors interrupting them.

"Jolly good," Hastings said.

"By the way," I said. "How do you know about my father and this Ivory Lady?"

"Informants."

"Why don't your informants just tell you J.A.'s location?"

"That's the one thing J.A. has kept a closely guarded secret."

"How did you survive?" Capi asked.

"I almost didn't. Like I said, Baako found me. He took me to his village. Then I followed him to this valley where..."

I grabbed Jama's hands. "You can't believe what I saw." She gripped my hands tighter. I turned my attention to the others. I described the massacre of the elephants. How Baako's warriors killed the poachers.

"There was a white man directing the slaughter."

Hastings leaned forward. "Do you know his name?"

I nodded. "Yates. Percy Yates."

Hastings said, "We know about him. He's one of your father's men."

"He claimed he was only a middleman," I said.

Hastings twirled his moustache. "Nonsense. Yates is J.A.'s righthand man. Believe me, Yates knows exactly where J.A.'s compound is."

Ngari thought for a minute. "Did Yates know you were J.A.'s son?"

I shook my head. "No."

Hastings said, "J.A. will figure it out. Not many young white Americans show up at an ivory shoot in the middle of Africa?"

Ngari asked, "Where is Yates?"

"Baako's warriors tied him up and put him in the jeep I drove here in," I said.

Ngari went to the window. "Is that the jeep out there?"

'Yeah." I said. "But Yates isn't there. He got away from me at Narok."

"Tell us exactly what happened," Capi said.

"I just did," I said.

"Go over it again but this time try to remember every detail."

I tried to recall every sordid thing that happened. The massacre, how Baako's men killed the poachers, how we captured Yates. How Yates killed a baby elephant. That really bothered Jama. And how Yates gave me the slip in Narok. I didn't tell them about Baako's surgery on Yates. Then I remembered. The tally book. It was still in my back pocket.

"I forgot to tell you about this. I found it on Yates," I said.

I handed the book to Capi. Hastings and Ngari huddled around her. She flipped through the pages.

"This is a tally book," she said.

"That's what Yates called it," I said.

Hastings asked to examine it. Capi handed it to him. He and Ngari studied it. Hastings turned to me.

"Poachers use these books to record how much ivory they harvested," Hastings said.

"I wish people would stop using the word harvest," I said. "It's murder."

Capi stood, paced. "Did Yates say anything to you that could help us find your father?" she asked.

I shook my head. "No. We questioned him. Asked him who his boss was. He mentioned my father, but said he only had a phone number."

"What phone number?" Capi asked.

"It's in the back of that book," I said. "I called it."

"Who answered?" Capi said.

"My father."

Hastings asked, "Are you sure it was him?"

I nodded. "It was him."

Jama grabbed my hand and squeezed. I looked at her. Tears in her eyes.

Hastings thumbed to the phone number.

He turned to Ngari. "We need to find where this phone is located. It doesn't look like a local number. Do you recognize it?"

Ngari studied it. "No. Could be in Tanganyika. I have a cousin who lives in Dar es Salaam. I'll call him."

Ngari picked up the phone on Cole's desk, dialed a number. We waited. Someone on the other end answered. Ngari said, "Hello. Mburu. Is that you?" Ngari put a finger in his ear. "Yes. Yes, it's Ngari. Speak up." His eyes shifted to us then to the phone. "I have a question for you." Ngari held out his hand for the tally book. Hastings gave it to him. Ngari cradled the phone between his shoulder and neck. He found the last page in the book. "Listen to this phone number." He read the number slowly. Waited, repeated it. "Is it a local number in Tanganyika?" Ngari listened, his brow wrinkled. Nodded. "Okay. Okay, cousin. Thank you." He hung up. "He said it was a Tanganyika number, but he didn't know the area where it might be located."

"Try the Kenyan phone company," Capi said. "They might know."

Ngari dialed a number. Spoke with someone for a minute. Hung up.

"They consider Tanganyika a foreign country. They have no information on foreign telephone exchanges," he said.

Hastings stroked his chin. "Well, we're sure J.A. wouldn't operate out of the cities like Arusha or Dar es Salaam. Too high profile. No, it has to be an out-of-the-way place."

Capi considered Hasting's comment. "Somewhere remote. A place where J.A. could ship large amounts of ivory out of the country undetected."

"Exactly," Hastings said.

"Moving that much ivory by truck would be very time-consuming and too much exposure," Ngari said. "Transporting it out of the country by air would be the only option. Warden, is it possible that's the way they're moving the ivory?"

Hastings shrugged. "I presume."

The word Hastings spoke triggered a thought, a memory.

"What did you say?" I asked.

"I beg your pardon."

"You said presume." I gave it my best English accent. "As in 'Doctor Livingstone, I presume.'"

Capi, Hastings, Ngari exchanged puzzled glances.

Hastings said, "Son, have you gone daft?"

"I'm sorry. It brings back memories."

I paused a moment to collect my thoughts.

"When I was a boy, my father read a lot of adventure books to me. My favorite was Henry Morton Stanley's book How I Found Livingston."

Hastings glared at me. "What on earth does that have to do with finding J.A. Quill?"

They all gave me a strange look.

"It's makes sense," I said. "The tally book, the phone number in Tanganyika. Someplace remote." I turned to Hastings. "When you said the word presume, I remembered the maps in Stanley's book. There was this big lake in Tanganyika."

Ngari interrupted. "Lake Tanganyika."

"Yes," I said. "The village where Stanley found Livingston. It's on Lake Tanganyika. And very remote. A place so remote, transporting tons of ivory would go completely undetected."

Hastings was getting impatient. "Get to the point, boy."

Ngari and I exchanged glances and laughed.

Together we said, "Ujiji."

36.

HASTINGS BELLOWED, "UJIJI?"

Ngari broke in, excited. He knew instantly what I was talking about.

"Yes," he said, "Ujiji. I've been there. Very famous. It's where Stanley found Livingston. The story is known to all African school children."

Not wanting to be outdone, Hastings added, "And to British students as well." He turned to Ngari. "They were both English you know."

Ngari gave Hastings a disapproving look. "Yes, sir. And they both became famous in Africa."

Hastings gave Ngari a "Harrumph."

Ngari said, "Our patrols have pushed most of the poachers out of our national parks in Kenya, including J.A.'s enterprise. So, where else would he go but to Uganda or Tanganyika? Neither country has comprehensive anti-poaching programs. It's perfect territory for poaching."

I asked them, "Are there lots of elephants in Tanganyika?"

Hastings spoke. "The country has the greatest concentration of wildlife in East Africa. Especially elephant herds."

Ngari added, "There are millions of pounds of ivory in Tanganyika to be harvested." Ngari remembered my objection to that word. "I mean to be illegally appropriated." He smiled at me. I shrugged approval.

Hastings played with his moustache. "If Quill has moved his operations to Ujiji, how would we find him? He could set up operations anywhere in the area. Are there any local police we can contact?"

Ngari said, "I doubt it. It's a small village. Very remote. But even if there was a police presence, you can bet J.A. has them on his payroll."

I thought a moment. I looked at Ngari.

"You mentioned one way to move that much ivory would be by air. And, as you said, there's Lake Tanganyika."

For the second time, Ngari and I exchanged glances. "Seaplanes," we said in unison.

Hastings became enthusiastic. "Seaplanes would be the most efficient way. And seaplanes would also be the most logical method for our attack." He moved to the wall map of East Africa behind Cole's desk, tracing a straight line with his finger from Nairobi to Lake Tanganyika. "We fly in at night, land here about a mile south of Ujiji with a half a dozen troops, go in by foot. When we find him, we hit him first thing the next morning."

Capi said, "Before we go flying off to Tanganyika, we have to first make sure Ujiji is J.A.'s base of operations. We must be right about this because if our intelligence is correct, he'll be meeting with the Ivory Lady any day now. Once that happens, she pays him off, flies the ivory out of the country and J.A. disappears forever. We only have one shot at this."

Hastings said, "Then Ujiji it is. It seems the only logical place for his operations. We have to take the chance that is where he is located."

Capi, along with Ngari and Hastings, gathered around the wall map to plan the expedition. If my theory about my father's whereabouts proved correct, I felt I might get my wish to see him again, but not in the way I had planned.

Capi told Jama they were going to be busy for a while planning the operation. In the meantime, she should take me to dinner.

We got reservations at The Lord Delamere Restaurant. My appearance wasn't exactly up to the standards of what Jama said was a world class restaurant. I excused myself, went to my basement room, freshened up and quickly changed clothes. I didn't show up in a tuxedo, but I was sort of presentable.

I hadn't eaten a decent meal in days. After all I had been through, to sit down to a fancy dinner in a fancy hotel with Jama was, to say the least, beyond anything I could have dreamed. Right away, I asked the server if the restaurant served hamburgers and french fries. Before he could answer, Jama laughed and ordered fish and chips for me, saying it was the closest thing they had to french fries. She ordered something called masala chai. It was the color of tomato soup. She finished with something she called pialu which was rice and beef. For a drink, she ordered wine. As for me, a Coca Cola.

"Do you and your mother live in Nairobi?" I asked.

"Yes," Jama said. "We live in the white section."

"Where do the native Africans live?"

"Well, they're not really allowed to live in Nairobi. It's so unfair when you think this is their country."

"I know what you mean. We have the same problem back home. It's just as unfair where I live."

Jama sipped her wine. "Jack, when you came halfway around the world to find your father, what did you expect?"

I dove into my fish and chips. She was right about the chips being like french fries. But the fish was no substitute for a cheeseburger.

"What do you mean?" I asked.

"Well, you hadn't seen him in so many years and now that you've learned what business he's in..."

"You mean that he's a criminal?"

"I know this is tough for you. I just hate to see you get hurt."

I picked at the chips left on my plate.

"I was hurt by him a long time ago, Jama."

"But are you ready to see him arrested or even worse?"

"You mean killed?"

She looked away.

"You know," she said, "you don't have to do this. Maybe it's best if you go home. Forget about him."

My eyebrows raised. "Are you trying to get rid of me?"

She smiled. "No. Actually, I'd like it if you stayed. I was simply thinking what is in store for your father might make Africa a place of bad memories."

That made me laugh. "Bad memories travel with you wherever you go. But I've got some good memories to go home with. I'm here with them right now."

She reached across the table and took my hand. "So," she said, taking a sip of wine, "are you going with them to Ujiji?"

"Of course."

"And you're prepared for what might happen?"

"Now you're trying to scare me into not going."

She leaned forward. A serious look in her eyes. "Jack, I hate to be so blunt but going on this operation is a lose-lose situation for you."

"I don't think of it in terms of losing. Just trying to close out a chapter in my life."

"Well, if you go, be careful. These people. Your father, that is. It's my understanding he is a ruthless man and will do anything to get what he wants."

"You sound like my Aunt Edith," I said.

"She knows what she's talking about."

"Look, I don't know how all of this is going to turn out. But I've got to go with them. If I could have one moment with my dad. One more moment just to look into his eyes to see if there's still something of a trace of what he used to be. That would mean a lot to me."

"I thought you came here to make him pay for what he did to your mother."

I stood. Leaned over and kissed her.

I told her, "Thanks for dinner. I have to get ready."

When I got to Cole's office, they had finished planning the operation. Hastings informed me the Americans loaned them a Grumman SHU-16 Albatross, an American-made float plane large enough for at least a dozen people, capable of landing on land or water. Ngari said his contingent included six rangers, members of the 3rd Battalion Kenya Rifles. They will be joined by himself, Warden Hastings and Capi Lewis.

"What about me?" I asked.

Warden Hastings, his attention locked on the map. "Sorry, kid. No civilians on this trip."

I marched up to him. Got in his face.

"I'm going, Hastings, and that's that."

Capi was also studying the map. She gave me a warning look. Hastings came to attention like the soldier he was.

"Young man, I am an officer in the King's African Rifles and this is a military operation. Civilians are strictly forbidden from engaging in military exercises involving possible combat scenarios."

"Have you ever seen my father?" I asked.

He went stiff-necked. "Not to my knowledge."

I turned to Ngari. "Have you, sir?"

He shook his head.

"And you, Capi. You don't know what he looks like either, do you?"

"No. As I told you, I think I only met him once."

I faced Hastings. "If you plan to capture or kill him, don't you want to know if you've got the real J.A. Quill? Or would you rather have some double he planted so he could escape to poach again?"

The three looked at each other. Ngari shrugged. Capi held out her hands in surrender. Hastings faced me, arms folded, stern face.

"Alright, young man. Now you listen to me. If we allow you on this trip, you will do exactly as I say. Understand?"

"Yes sir."

"You will stay on the plane at all times until we complete the campaign. Do you hear me?"

I stood at attention and saluted him.

"Yes sir," I said.

He examined me as if he were inspecting one of his soldiers. Out of habit, he returned my salute. My ROTC training kicked in. I stood at attention, waiting to be dismissed. He ignored me.

He said to Capi, "He's now your responsibility, Mrs. Lewis."

He turned to study the map. Like the good soldier I was, I continued to stand at attention. Capi shook her head and chuckled.

Finally, I was going to see my father.

37.

THE GRUMMAN TOOK OFF from Nairobi airport at 3:30 a.m. It was a big, loud plane. Because the stakes were so high for J.A. in trying to sell tons of illicit ivory and get away with a fortune, Hastings expected him to have a small army protecting his interests. We came prepared for a tough fight.

There were ten people packed into the Grumman cabin. Six commandos, Capi, Ngari, Hastings and me. The combat soldiers were dressed in black gear equipped with various weapons. Rifles, handguns, grenades, knives. They wore slouch hats plus heavy boots. If we landed on water, there were rubber boats ready to take us ashore.

Ngari planned to go into the village with Capi to question the locals. He wore civilian clothing. Capi dressed in a safari outfit, no weapons, a cloth hat. As for Hastings, he was decked out in the same outfit as the soldiers. He wore a nickel-plated General Patton WW II revolver. Since I was to stay on the plane, I wore my usual safari jacket, khaki pants, flannel shirt, Aussie hat and my sneakers. I wasn't allowed guns or knives.

As we climbed into the clouds, the Grumman motors were so loud it made conversation difficult. Hastings huddled with Capi and Ngari over a map of the planned attack. Hastings believed the notorious Ivory Lady, Mrs. Chen, would either use a seaplane or barges to transport the illicit ivory from J.A.'s operations in Ujiji to a Burundi port a hundred miles north. The cargo would be off-loaded in the city of Bujumbura and flown out of their new airport to China. But Capi continued to remind him there was still no proof J.A.'s operations were in Ujiji.

Hastings turned to Ngari.

"Did you find out anything from your contacts in Bujumbura?"

Ngari shouted over the engine noise. "There are shipments of ivory due to come into the port at Usumbura from the south. My contact doesn't know who's behind the shipments or when they will arrive."

"Does he know from what city on the lake the shipments are coming from?" Hastings asked.

"Yes," Ngari said, looking at Capi. "The ship manifests list the origin of the shipments as Ujiji."

"Could it be legitimate ivory coming out of Ujiji?"

Ngari shook his head. "Not sure. But my contact said the manifest only lists a company name he's never heard of."

"What name?" Capi asked.

Ngari searched his jacket. Pulls out a piece of paper. Reads, "M.J. Enterprises."

It took a second for the name to sink in. When it hit me, I shouted, "Did you say M.J. Enterprises?"

Ngari studied his notes again. "Yes."

"That's got to be my father's company."

Hastings said, "How do you know?"

"It all fits," I said, raising my voice. "My mother's name was Molly Jean. Her initials were M.J."

Capi sat up straight. Took a deep breath. Ngari looked at Hastings and smiled.

Hastings nodded. "It appears Mister J.A. Quill is about to get a surprise visit."

Capi said, "I hate to be a spoil sport but now that we are pretty sure J.A. is operating out of Ujiji, we still don't know where his operation is physically located. We need to find out exactly where his compound is before we go barreling into the area?"

Hastings said, "Correct. Our only hope of finding it is to question the locals as to his whereabouts. Chances are J.A. has an elaborate residence somewhere in the area. You can bet the villagers know where it is." He turned to Ngari and Capi. "Your assignment is to find it."

The over 500-hundred-mile trip from Nairobi to Ujiji took about two-and-a-half hours. The sun was coming up just as we reached the shoreline of Lake Tanganyika. Hastings ordered the pilot to turn north along the eastern shore of the lake. He wanted to see if there were any seaplanes in the area or barges already underway.

At the altitude we were flying, boats appeared as small dots. But we were looking for big objects like barges or ships or airplanes. The port Hastings was looking for was at Kigoma, Ujiji's sister city. When we made a pass over the port of Kigoma, Hastings shouted at the pilot to circle back.

Hastings pointed at the port. There was a lengthy object tied to a wharf. An open barge filled with what appeared to be white objects. Hastings ordered the pilot to go lower. When we were directly over the barge, Hastings jumped out of his seat.

"There. See it?" he roared. "That is a cargo of ivory."

A long, flat-bottomed barge loaded with stacks of tusks glistened in the morning sun.

"So much for transporting the ivory out by seaplane," Ngari added.

Hastings directed the pilot to keep going south. About five minutes later, he spotted the area where he wanted the plane to land. We made a U-turn and started a slow descent. The plane hugged the shoreline, splashing down about a mile south of port Kigoma and Ujiji.

Before the engines died, two members of the attack team inflated one of the rubber rafts and tossed it into the lake. The men helped Capi and Ngari into the boat. Capi motioned to me to join them.

"I thought you wanted me to stay on the plane," I said.

"Jack, if it hadn't been for you, we'd still be guessing where your father is," Capi said. "You're coming with us."

Hastings nodded his approval.

38.

THE AREA WHERE WE landed was in a wide cove about a mile from Ujiji. The plane stopped about half a mile from a small fishing village. We could see lights dancing on the water. Ngari said the glow came from pressure lamps attached to the bows of fishermen's boats.

We were concerned the approach of the plane might have spooked the fishermen. We wanted our arrival to remain as secretive as possible until we had a chance to find out where J.A.'s compound was located.

Time was of the essence. Hastings gave instructions to question the locals about large structures in the area that could be J.A.'s compound. He and the others would wait on the plane until we finished our assignment.

Capi, Ngari and I stepped on shore as the first rays of sun hit the beach. Two curious women immediately confronted us. They were giggling and chattering in their native language. Ngari seemed to understand them. He engaged in conversation, smiling, nodding his head and being the charming stranger asking for information. They were obviously flirting with him. And one of the younger women kept making inviting gestures to me.

Capi gave us a look. "I think they were propositioning you guys."

We grinned, shrugged. Ngari said, "You misunderstood, Mrs. Lewis. They were simply telling me they knew nothing of an American who lived in Ujiji."

Capi laughed. "My Swahili isn't that rusty."

He got serious. "Anyway, we quickly must move inland. We have a lot of ground to cover and not much time."

We headed north toward the main villages of Ujiji and Kigoma. The shore was lined with palm trees. Beyond the village were thick green forests rising into the surrounding mountains. Ngari went in the opposite direction looking for information. Capi and I headed into the main village of Ujiji. When we reached the center of town, villagers crowded around us, some begging for food, others just curious. Mostly, we were ignored by the hundreds of people gathered in markets, coming and going out of thatched huts, bringing fish in from the lake. There were a few cars and trucks moving about with people hanging on doors and bumpers. Capi spotted a group of English hunters loading a dead kudu into a beat-up truck. She pulled me aside behind a hut. She said we didn't want to run into any whites tied to J.A.

Ngari eventually caught up with us.

"Hurry," he said, out of breath, excited. "We must move quickly." He was already jogging toward the boats. "I'll explain when we get onboard."

Once on the plane, Ngari closed the hatch and told Hastings, "We need to get in the air now." Hastings ordered the pilot to start the engines.

"What's going on?" Hastings asked.

Ngari said he questioned a few locals about big houses in the nearby mountains. One of them, an old man, asked Ngari why he wanted to know. Ngari made up a story he had a delivery to make but couldn't find the house. The old man said to ask his son. He had worked at a house in the hills to the north. He called his son over. When Ngari asked the boy about the house, he grew nervous. Ngari pressed him for more information. The boy said the house was about ten miles north of Ujiji up in the mountains. But when Ngari questioned him about the barge in the port loaded with ivory, the boy abruptly turned and ran away.

Back at the plane, Ngari told Hastings, "The good news is we now know the general location where J.A.'s compound is. The bad news is he probably knows we're here."

Hastings hurried to the cockpit to speak to the pilot. The pilot revved the Grumman to takeoff speed, wheeled the plane south, and we climbed to the clouds. The plane took a U headed north over the lake. Minutes later, we were circling a mountainside just above a small village on the lakeshore. I was the first to spot the house above the village.

This was no ordinary house. This was a mansion. It appeared to be a two-story structure with a balcony wrapped around the upper floor. A courtyard dotted with lounge chairs. Umbrellas circled a large swimming pool. Surrounding the house, an acre of smooth green lawn protected by a white stone fence. All of this sat on top of a mountain in a vast area of dense forest. The sun was high enough to reflect off a river running behind and below the property to the east.

The pilot flew north, turned south again, and started his descent. As we slowed to land, we could see off to our left the huts of a small village. People swarmed out of the huts, running toward the shore, pointing at the plane.

Hastings said, "So much for surprise."

The commandos hurried to get ready. Loaded guns, checked equipment. Hastings told the pilot to bypass the village and stop a mile south. The plane came to rest about a hundred yards from a beach. Capi and Ngari had already changed into combat gear. Capi grabbed a weapon. It was a machine gun. She saw my surprise.

I said, "I thought you were just a volunteer."

"Now you know my secret," she said.

The commandos wasted no time launching three inflatable boats. Hastings told me to stay with the plane. Under no circumstances was I to follow. I objected. He ignored me.

Capi, Hastings and Ngari followed the commandos out the door. I watched as they made their way to shore. They dragged the boats into a thicket, covered them with bushes, then disappeared into a jungle. Moments later, villagers swarmed onto the beach gesturing wildly at the Grumman. They had guns.

What happened next scared the hell out of me. The villagers started to fire at us. The plane was about a hundred yards from the beach. Bullets started hitting the plane. The loud thunks told me these guys had some powerful rifles. Nothing you would expect from locals in a small remote village. I heard the Grumman engines turn over. The pilot was getting the hell out of there. He never made it. A bullet smashed through the window, hitting him in the head. He slumped over. The plane went out of control. It veered toward the beach. More bullets pierced the windows. Time for me to bail.

I opened the door on the opposite side of the beach. Dove into the water. Swam fast as I could to get away before a bullet pierced the gas tanks and the plane exploded. I dove deep. Swam for as long as I could without surfacing. Then the gas tanks blew. Even underwater, the blast was deafening. The shock wave rushed by me like a hurricane. One of the plane's propellers hit the water about ten yards from me. Swimming underwater, I watched the giant propeller slowly sink to the bottom. More debris rained down before I surfaced far from shore. The only thing left of the plane was a burning hulk, one propeller on fire, still spinning, the skeleton of the Grumman beached like a wounded whale. The locals on shore raised their weapons, cheering. I was definitely outside the tourist zone.

I treaded water for about five minutes. I was sure the attackers hadn't seen me. They finally headed toward their village. I hoped they hadn't spotted Hastings and company when they landed on the beach. There were too many villagers for them to handle.

39.

IF EVER THERE WAS a time to be smart, now was the time to be smarter.

I studied the coastline. Clear of locals. As I swam toward the beach, I heard more gunfire. When I reached shore, I hurried into the woods as fast as I could.

A volley of shots came from the direction of the village. Sounded like a small war. When the commandos heard the plane explode, they must have figured the villagers had something to do with it. They probably headed to the village to take control of the locals before scaling the mountain to fight whatever forces J.A. had waiting for them.

My curiosity overruled smart. I headed toward the village, not knowing what I would find. If the native population had somehow overwhelmed the commandos, I was a dead man. It seemed unlikely given the half-clad, unorganized appearance of the mob that blew up the Grumman.

Making my way through the forest would have been easy enough. I confronted more than trees. Walls of thorny underbrush, ravines, rocky barriers. The woods were silent. I checked every step I took not to cause any undue noise.

When I reached the village clearing, all I saw were circles of huts. No people milling about. Then I saw the bodies. Several men lay in pools of blood. Weapons scattered around the fallen. No commandos in sight. No doubt Hastings and his crack troops had no problems with the inexperienced villagers. I wondered if their attack on the plane was to defend against foreign invaders or were they hired by J.A. to protect his mountain retreat?

Distant gunfire came from the mountaintop above the village. The commandos had obviously reached my father's hilltop fortress. Before I joined them, I found a submachine gun among the bodies. It appeared to be new and fully loaded. I had no idea how to operate it. I checked to see if there was a safety. Found something I thought was a safety. Pushed on it. Then aimed the weapon at the lake and pulled the trigger. It jumped in my hands, spraying a few bullets over the water. On-the-job training. Works every time.

I had to hurry. The idea of coming all this way from Virginia to bury another family member drove me to breakneck speed. Even though I had planned to force my father to answer for his cruelty to my mother, I didn't want to see him dead. I charged up terrain so steep it took all my effort to make it to the top.

When I reached the compound, a full-blown battle was underway. The commandos were dug in around a stone wall, firing into the building. The building was more impressive than it had appeared from the air. Two stories, tile roof, white stucco walls. Open view windows wrapped around both levels. Balconies and a rooftop view of the valley below. Whoever built this monstrosity meant to protect it from the air and ground.

Hastings moved among his troops, shouting orders. Capi hunched down, protected by the wall. A commando raised up to fire only to be hit by a shot to the shoulder. Ngari ran to him. Checked him out. The man waved him away, stood, and continued fighting. They were too busy to notice me. Just as I was about to make myself known, Hastings saw me.

He ran to me. "We heard the explosion. What happened to the plane?"

"The villagers blew it up," I shouted over the gunfire.

"Stay here. We're about to stage an attack."

He gathered his commandos, pointing them in different directions. Half went one way, half the other. Hastings, nickel-plated revolver drawn, breached the stone fence heading into a hail of rapid fire coming from the house. Ngari followed. I peeked over the wall. Several figures inside the house were shooting from windows, peppering the ground beneath Hastings and Ngari. They bolted for the mansion. Ngari stopped midway to take a shot at a man coming at them. I noticed a shooter at one of the windows. He had a bead on Ngari. I raised the machine gun. Aimed dead center at the man and pulled the trigger. A spray of bullets found their mark. The man dropped his rifle, falling out of the window onto the concrete below. Ngari turned. Looked surprised at what I had done. I shrugged. He gave me a salute then moved on.

I wondered where my father was. I decided against storming the castle. Instead, I circled around, following the lead of one of the commando groups. J.A.'s men must have spotted me from the house. A couple of bullets zinged past me after ricocheting off the stone wall. I scrambled around the property eventually coming to an entry point. Three of the commandos sprinted ahead of me through the opening, climbing a row of stone steps up to the house three at a time. A dozen rounds danced at their feet. They moved into the courtyard, heading inside the mansion. I followed.

The interior of the house was like something I'd never seen. An enormous chandelier hung above a vast living room. Banks of tall windows framed in expensive looking drapes. Cushy sofas, chairs, a glass coffee table, potted trees, large paintings, a winding staircase, and a skylight bigger than most houses. I recalled the modest house we had lived in before my father abandoned us. He'd come a long way since being an oyster shucker and shoveling shit at a zoo.

An explosion shattered most of the windows. Glass flew everywhere. Hastings and Ngari, followed by Capi, jumped through one of the broken windows. When they got to the middle of the room, men upstairs fired at them from a balcony. Hastings and Ngari returned fire hitting two of the men. They fell into the dining room.

Shouting from the second floor, sounds of running, doors slamming shut. All six of the commandos joined forces led by Hastings, Ngari, and

Capi. They charged up the winding staircase, firing as they climbed. I followed, not having any idea how I was going to help. I couldn't stand around staring at fixtures.

When I got to the second floor, Hastings and company were rushing down a hallway, stopping at an enormous set of double doors. As they approached, muzzle blasts from behind the doors followed by a dozen holes ripping through the heavy wood, barely missed Hastings and Ngari. Capi hid behind an open doorway. A round dug into the wall about a foot from my head.

A commando wedged a hand grenade over one of the handles to the big door. Pulled the pin and took cover. The doors shattered in a cloud of splintered wood. A woman on the other side screamed.

Hastings, Ngari, and the commandos barged through the opening. Three of the enemy inside returned fire only to be shot dead by the commandos. I waited a moment before entering the room. I heard loud cursing in a language unknown to me. I entered the room to see Ngari behind a small woman, holding her arms. She was dressed in a gown, her hair gussied up like she was going to the opera. She kicked Ngari in the leg, calling him names.

Capi entered the room. She slung her machine gun over her shoulder, approached the woman. Searched her for weapons. The woman pulled an arm free, slapped at Capi, but Capi was too quick for her. She grabbed the woman's wrist, twisted it, causing the woman to cry out in pain.

"You're not a very nice girl, are you?" Capi said in her proper English accent.

Hastings faced the woman. "So, you're the Ivory Lady we've heard so much about."

She spit in his face. He laughed. Took out a handkerchief. Wiped it away. He looked around.

"Where's Mr. Quill?"

She spoke in broken English. "You have made big mistake. I am Chinese citizen and a guest in your country. I do nothing wrong. You have no right to hold me."

Hastings turned to Ngari. "Search the house. We need to find J.A. before he escapes."

Ngari motioned to the commandos to follow him. They ran through the door and down the hall searching all the upstairs rooms. I waited as Capi and Hastings continued to grill the Ivory Lady about ivory shipments, her agreements with J.A., any paperwork she might have. She clammed up, so I followed Ngari to do my own search.

Several doors were open. Dead bodies, weapons, equipment scattered throughout the rooms. I moved to the balcony overlooking the downstairs living area. Just as I was about to search one of the big rooms, I caught sight of a figure running out of the house, through the courtyard, across the lawn. Whoever it was headed straight for the forest behind the compound. The runner got to the opening in the stone fence, turned and looked back at the building.

It was my father. J.A. Quill.

40.

MY FIRST REACTION WAS to alert Hastings. Then the thought hit me. This was my one chance to confront my father. Alone. The reason I had come to Africa. My opportunity to do what I promised my mother over her grave. To find him and make him pay.

I flew down the stairs, out of the building, going for the woods where my father disappeared. I hadn't gone too far when I came to the side of the mountain. The hill was so steep I lost my footing and almost fell. Trying to negotiate a forty-five-degree slope is tough enough, but to do it through a stand of trees is twice as difficult. I slipped several times. Almost slammed into a few trees. Momentarily lost the trail. I tried to find a sign of Dad. I caught sight of movement ahead, through the underbrush. I ran toward it. Took a right turn past a rock outcropping into a mess of thorns, ripping my shirt, drawing blood. I backtracked, found the trail, then sprinted through a group of palm trees.

Just as I entered a grassy clearing, I caught sight of my father entering the woods on the other side. The clearing leveled out. I got across quickly only to hit another downhill grade. I'm not sure how long I chased him. Saw him several times. He was pretty far ahead. I negotiated several twists and turns, dense trees, open fields, a tricky angle covered with gravel. Finally, I emerged from a rock gorge to the banks of a river.

The river ran down through a valley. It was wide, the rushing water deep and swift. To get across meant either wading or crossing on a series of rocks.

I looked to the other side. No sign of him. If he made it across, he had obviously negotiated a bridge of slippery stones. I was so far behind him if I didn't hurry, I'd lose him.

I tried to find my footing on a flat slab of rock near the shore. I took the chance, put my full weight on it, moved forward and slipped. I fell waist high into the water. Leaned on my gun to gain my balance. Grabbed the rock. The water pushed hard against me.

I was about to wade across when a shot rang out. A bullet ricocheted off a nearby boulder. Couldn't believe my father was shooting at me. I figured he didn't know it was me. I tried to locate him, but he was probably hiding in the trees.

I let go my grip on the slab. Another rock, not too far ahead. I fought the river surge. Almost took me under. Reached for the next foothold. Climbed up on the rock. In the attempt, the gun slipped out of my hand. Grabbed for it but it was gone.

The other side was yards away. Another shot. The bullet zinged off the rock I stood on. I almost lost balance again. Spotted another rock about four feet away. A long jump. Determined, I gathered my strength, took a deep breath, lunged. I fell short. Hit the rock chest first.

I was stunned. I slipped beneath the surface of the water. Sunlight danced in the swirling rapids. I grasped for something, anything. My fingernails grabbed a stone and came up with a fistful of moss. I was losing it, being swept away. Bubbles rushed from my mouth. I grabbed wildly. Caught something solid. Pulled my head above water. Choking, spitting, sucking air. I clung to a big bolder. I struggled against a cold chunk of granite. Pushed up with everything I had. My knees hurt so bad they almost buckled. I stood, dripping wet, cold but upright. Water up to my chest. Cleared my eyes, got my bearings. I still had a long way to go to the other side.

And there he was. Standing across the river.

My father, on the other side, staring at me as if he'd never laid eyes on me. Years since I last saw him. He had a beard. His hair was long and gray. He wore black slacks and a fancy white shirt. A bowtie hung half off his collar. He was holding a rifle.

"Dad?"

"Go home, Jack."

He raised the rifle. Aimed directly at me. I could see his finger on the trigger. He didn't flinch. His expression, desperate, foreign to me. Memories flooded my mind. Baseball games, birthdays, days at the zoo. Books he read to me. The dreams of adventure we shared. Then, the day he left. The man, once my hero, simply walked away, never to return, leaving a boy to wonder what he'd done to deserve this.

I held out my arms in surrender.

He hesitated. Stared at me. Dropped the rifle and ran.

There was no time to wade through the rapids. Swimming was the quickest way across. I dove into the water, trying to avoid the stones. The swift water continued to push me downstream. I kept bumping into boulders. I shoved against the current as hard as I could. Finally, I reached shore. I stood and stepped onto the other side of the river.

I found the rifle where he dropped it. I figured he might meet up with someone who had a weapon. I had no idea what waited for me at the end of the chase. I picked up the rifle and went after him.

Another grove of closely packed trees. As I dodged in and out through the maze, I caught flashes of him. More bushes. Granite outcroppings. My wounds from the thorn bushes ached. I was almost out of breath. The rifle was getting heavy. I kept it anyway, pushing forward through bushes, trees, ravines.

I broke through a forest into a clearing. Ahead, a sheer rockface split by a narrow crevice. I was exhausted. Took a moment to catch my breath. I was afraid my father had gotten away when I heard the sound of something crashing through underbrush followed by the loud trumpet call of an elephant. I headed for the break in the wall. Another scream only this time it was human. It was my father.

On the other side of the wall, a frightening scene. A massive bull elephant had my father pinned against a mound of earth, its tusks buried on either side of him as its giant head pushed against his chest. Dad screamed in pain. The bull withdrew, throwing its tusk in the air and letting out another brassy scream.

"Dad," I yelled. He looked at me.

"Shoot him, goddamnit. Shoot him."

It was too late. The bull charged again. This time, one of his tusks pierced my father's chest. The sound of crunching bones. Blood gushed. J.A. screamed in agony.

When the bull pulled back, ready for another charge, I ran between him and my father. If I had any hope of saving him, I had to stop a third charge. My move seemed to surprise the giant. It started to rock, twisting its trunk, unsure of my intentions. It gave me a strange look as if to say this doesn't involve you. I glanced at my father. His shirt, blood-soaked. I could hear the gurgling in his chest. His eyes cut to me. His expression was desperate, chilling. He tried to speak but blood gushed from his mouth.

I was only a few feet from the giant, still holding the rifle at a ready position. I stared directly into his eyes. The old bull had probably seen a lot of guns like the one I was holding. Guns that had killed too many of his kind. I didn't come to Africa to make my father pay with his life. But the last thing I wanted to do was to make this creature pay for his for what my father had done to thousands like him.

I recalled my encounter with another elephant. I dropped the rifle and held my arms high, making a friendly push-back motion. I spoke to it quietly, calmly in low tones letting him know that I was not a threat. It let out a low rumble, its ears flapping. Then it did something strange. It moved slowly toward me stopping within an arm's length. I didn't know what to do so I did something crazy. I reached out and put my hand on its trunk.

I suppose most people would think this creature's encounter with my father was pure coincidence. My father was at the wrong place at the wrong time. But I had a feeling it was divine intervention that brought them face to face. The collective remembrance of the thousands of elephants from Kilimanjaro to the Great Rift Valley filled with the brothers and sisters of this magnificent bull that had suffered so much misery at the hands of humans like my father. I believe they all knew. They all remembered. They all carried the collective memories of the horror, the carnage, the deaths they had suffered at hands of human beings. Was this their moment of revenge? I don't think so. This was their shared moment of justice. That's when I finally understood the difference between justice and revenge. And I wanted nothing more to do with revenge.

To my surprise, the bull ran its trunk over my arm, my shoulder, my head searching for something. Then threw its trunk in the air and let out a single, piercing trumpet call. Keeping its eyes on me it quietly withdrew, turned and walked away.

I hurried to my father. Knelt beside him. His lungs filled with blood. The gash in his chest, an open wound. He tried to smile but it wouldn't hold. He closed then opened his eyes. Looked at me as if to see me for the first time. Reached for my hand. Squeezed it. With the last of his strength, he motioned me closer. I pressed near him, listening. As I felt the breath leaving his body, he struggled to speak. A shadow passed over his eyes like a cloud over the sun. His words cracked, sputtered. As the light in his eyes was dying, he focused on me and smiled. He said, "Doctor Livingstone, I presume?"

Then he was gone.

As I stood over my father's lifeless body, all the heartaches he had caused disappeared like smoke from a dying fire. Nothing but memories flickering in the ashes of time.

41.

I WAS WAITING ON the tarmac at the Nairobi Airport for Capi and Jama to show up. I was not going to leave without seeing them. The British Airways jet was scheduled for takeoff at noon. I had my ticket and pack ready for the flight home. Finally, Capi came running up to me as if she hadn't seen me in years. Gave me a big hug.

"Where have you been, Jack? When we got back to Nairobi, you just disappeared. Jama was worried about you."

"I wasn't in much of a mood to visit."

She frowned. "I'm sorry about your father."

"Thanks," I said.

"But what we accomplished with your help was to shut down one of the biggest poaching operations in the history of Africa. The Ivory Lady is in prison for a very long stay."

"I'm afraid it's not going to end there," I said.

She looked at the clouds. "You're right. The more elephants we lose, the price of ivory goes up. I'm afraid the poaching will not end until all the elephants are gone." She put her hand on my shoulder. "You know, Warden Hastings and Ranger Ngari were very impressed with you. You have a job here with the Game Department anytime you want it."

"Thanks but I have to get home."

"What's the hurry? Got a girlfriend in Virginia?"

"Sort of," I said.

Capi frowned. "Jama is going to be very sad to hear that."

I laughed. "Jama has nothing to worry about. My girlfriend is an elephant."

"What?"

"Her name is Betty. We're very close."

"You have a thing for the big pachyderms, don't you?"

"Yeah. She's at the Virginia zoo. I worked there for Mr. Nagata and I promised him after I was finished with Africa, I would come home."

Capi thought for a minute. "I knew a man named Nagata. Was he ever here in Africa?"

"Yes. He and Mr. Cole were friends. That's why I looked Mr. Cole up when I got here. Mr. Nagata said he would help me."

She thought for a minute. "I remember him now. He had a nickname. We called him Blinky. He was a real item around here. Everybody knew Blinky. He was Cole's gunbearer. Then he left to go back to the States. He came back to Africa looking for animals for his zoo. As I remember, on one of his visits he bought an elephant. A female I think."

"That was probably my girl, Betty."

An announcement boomed over a loudspeaker. It was time for me to board my flight.

"Where's Jama?" I asked.

Capi looked at her watch. "She'll be here any minute. She doesn't want to miss you."

"Well, I'm not leaving without seeing her."

A minute later, Jama came out of the terminal. When she spotted me, she ran to me and gave me a big kiss.

"I thought you'd forgotten about me," I said.

She hugged me again. "How could I forget the man I love?"

I framed her face in my hands. "I love you too."

Jama blushed. "I wish I was going with you."

"Next time." I picked up my pack. "Well, it looks like I'm about to board. Capi, thanks for the ticket."

"After all you've done for us," she said, "it's the least the city of Nairobi could do for you."

Jama grabbed my arm. "I almost forgot."

She reached in her purse and brought out a wooden figure. It was in the shape of a bull elephant carved from dark brown wood with tusks white as ivory.

"This is beautiful," I said. "Where did you get this?"

"From a friend of yours," Jama said.

"What friend?"

She pointed to the end of the terminal. Standing on one leg, spear in hand, stood Baako. I smiled at him and held the carved elephant over my head in a gesture of thanks. Baako simply looked at me, aloof as ever.

A final boarding call for my plane. Jama wrapped her arms around me. Another kiss. I held her at arm's length. She was crying.

"Will you promise me you'll come back?" she said.

"I promise."

I kissed her for the last time. Hugged Capi. Said goodbye. Before I boarded, I turned and waved. Then I looked to the end of the terminal to wave goodbye to Baako.

He was gone.

THE END